i

Your lifejacket is under your seat.

Your lifejacket is under your seat

Your lifejacket is under your seat

But I can't find it. I am groping around under the seats and there is nothing here but sweet wrappers and empty plastic cups and a green sock. Perhaps green. In the murky light, it's not easy to tell. And why do I care? I should be thinking about getting out of here, not checking the colour of lost socks.

Your lifejacket is under your seat. That is definitely what she said.

Your lifejacket is under

Under water

You will soon be under water

You are under

Under your lifejacket

Your life is under

Your lifejacket is not under your seat. You have been lied to. My head hurts so badly and I am going to throw up again.

Your lifejacket is

Your lifejacket is

Orange!

Your orange is your lifejacket.

Your lifejacket is orange.

The flash of colour ahead of me clears the fog that has been swirling through my brain and for a brief moment the pain in my head abates and the nausea is held at bay. I see it now, poking out from under a seat a few rows ahead of me. I crawl slowly forward, suddenly aware that I am moving uphill and that the incline is getting steeper by the second. There is less water though. Is that a good thing? I hold onto the seats to prevent a backward slide; I don't know whether I would have the strength to get back here if that happens.

I reach my bright orange goal and pull it towards me. My vision blurs again and however much I rub my eyes, it refuses to clear. The world is grey and fuzzy, the only thing that stands out is the bright orange of the life-jacket. The nausea reaches critical levels and I turn my head quickly to the right so that, when I vomit, the lifejacket is not splattered. The movement sends a lance of pain across the front of my head and I let go of the seat and slide backwards into the water. It takes me weeks to crawl forward again and wedge myself between the seats. I keep my eyes closed as I pull the lifejacket on. There's something wrong. I thought they went over your head, but it has straps to slide my arms through. It feels small and uncomfortable and I wonder whether this one is designed for a child, but there is no time to look for another. Once it's on, I feel for the tape to secure it around my waist, but can't find it. Perhaps children's lifejackets are designed differently, but there's no time to find out. Keep moving. There is nothing I want more than to curl up and rest, but I push myself to keep going, one row at a time, towards the exit.

It's so hard to see. Shouldn't there be lights showing the way to the nearest exit? Isn't that what she said? I did pay attention, of course I did. After all, having gathered enough courage to board the plane, I was hardly going to ignore anything that might help me to survive in the event of a disaster. And this is definitely a disaster. But I don't see lights.

I see luggage and blankets and shoes and coffee cups and a laptop and dead people and

No, I do not see dead people. I will not see the dead people. I will see the door. There it is, just a few feet ahead of me. Sick. Feel so sick. This time, I don't get my head turned quickly enough. Vomit sprays everywhere, but I feel slightly better for a few moments.

There is an alarming sound, as though a giant is slurping the last few drops of milk-shake through a straw, and the angle of the floor tilts again until the rear of the plane is reaching into the sky and am holding on desperately to the seats to stop myself sliding back. Forcing my eyes open, I pull myself up, through the vomit, past the last few seats, towards the open back door. I pass the toilet and flash briefly to a vision of blood and glass, before hauling myself the last few inches to the doorway.

There is a silence that is somehow worse than the earlier noise and I know I have to get out now.

Shouldn't there be some kind of inflatable slide here? There is nothing, I am hovering above the sea, which is a million miles below me, and I pull myself to my feet, hanging onto the doorframe, bracing myself to jump. A scene from an early movie runs through my mind. There's a couple, standing by the railings on the deck of a sinking ship and someone is telling them that when they jump they should swim as far from the ship as they can before it goes down. He says that, when the ship finally goes down, anything close to it will be sucked down too. Did they jump? Did they survive? I have no idea. I don't even remember what the movie was called, or any other details. Just this. I must get as far as I can from the plane, as fast as I can.

The noise starts again and the plane is moving.

I close my eyes and leap outward, pushing hard with my legs, to get as much distance as possible from the plane.

I am amazed at how many thoughts can run though my head in the few seconds that it takes to reach the water. The human brain is pretty incredible, even when it's in pain and wobbling around like jelly inside a skull. I think about my travel insurance and wonder where the documents are. In the overhead luggage locker, probably. I realise that I didn't watch any of the in-flight movies and wonder whether I missed anything. I notice that I am only wearing one shoe. I wonder whether, if I throw up now, the vomit will hit the water before me, so that I land in it. Stephen Fry would know. I think that, when I get back, I will go onto the websites I searched before I left home and update them confirming that it's true, a plane will float for a short time if it lands on water. They said the pilot has to be very skilled to make that happen, though, so I guess we had a great pilot. I wonder whether he survived, whether he has children. By the time I hit the water, I am thinking that I forgot to leave a note with the cat food explaining that Oscar likes to eat separately from the others and will sulk if he's expected to share. Neither Ellie nor Dan feeds the cats often enough to remember. By the time my feet hit the water, my long, cotton dress has inverted itself, so that my legs are naked and my face is smothered by the soft cloth.

My momentum takes me under fast and it feels as though I have gone a long way down before I am able to slow myself and begin to work my way back towards the surface. On the way up, I am already reaching for the toggle that will inflate the lifejacket, but I can't find it. On the surface, I keep feeling around but it's not there and neither is the tube for manual inflation. There is something seriously wrong with this lifejacket. I feel a child's sense of injustice; I took so much time looking for this, while I was sick and in pain and now it doesn't work. I want to cry. I also want to throw up again, but I manage not to.

The sea is relatively calm. I start swimming, hampered by dress, which is now clinging to my legs and preventing them from separating properly, so that I have to work really hard with my arms in order to move forward. I would take it off, but that means taking off the life-jacket and I won't do that. I have no idea about direction, but I am gradually moving further from the plane, which has suddenly gone very quiet and is disappearing so slowly that I have a vision of someone with a giant winch, releasing it an inch at a time. I wish I had learned to do crawl, but I can only do breaststroke, which seems inadequately slow. I am moving away though. And then there's one last giant gurgle, as though the plugs in every bath in world have been pulled simultaneously, and the plane has gone and I am here, alone.

My head hurts. I would kill for a paracetamol. It's slightly better when I close my eyes, so I float for a while on my back, eyes closed, almost dozing. The nausea is better now and I am hoping I won't throw up again. Perhaps I could sleep for a while? It would be easy.

I do a mental shake and force my eyes open. With a useless lifejacket, if I fall asleep, I will drown. I look around. The sun is almost below the horizon behind me but there is still a little light. There is nothing to see but sea. Where is everybody else? They were clearly evacuated from the plane before I came round and managed to get out of the toilet, (well, except for the bodies, but there were not many of them and I don't want to think about that), but they can't have gone far. Do planes carry inflatable lifeboats? Have they already been picked up by a rescue boat? No, that's impossible. They can only have been a few minutes ahead of me, because otherwise the plane would have gone down before I could get out.

I turn slowly in the water, this time searching more carefully. And I hear something. A faint whistle. Then another. Lifejackets have whistles on them. Well, mine probably doesn't, mine seems to bear no resemblance to the one they showed us at the beginning of the flight at all. But others do. I peer into the failing light, in the direction of the sounds. The sun finally leaves for the day and now I see them. Tiny points of light, like fireflies, winking on and off in the distance. Your lifejacket has a light and a whistle. Really? Again, treading water, I slide my hands up and down the front of me and as far as I can to the back, and there's nothing there. But there are people over there. All I have to do is swim towards them. The winking is probably caused by the rise and fall of the waves. They are whistling to keep in contact, stay together.

I throw myself forward and start swimming.

The pain in my head returns so suddenly and so sharply that I cry out, causing me to swallow water and start to cough. I stop swimming, get my breathing under control again and rest, and the pain recedes. I need to move towards the others but I will have to do it slowly. I look round again, but now I can't see the lights. Turning slowly in the water, so that I don't exacerbate the nausea, I become panicked when I am sure I have completed two full revolutions and I haven't seen anything. They are too far away. I fumble uselessly with my lifejacket. Your lifejacket has a light and a whistle. I can't find them, and, to be honest, I feel as though the lifejacket is becoming heavier, pulling me down rather than buoying me up. My anxiety levels, perhaps dimmed by the pain and nausea, are suddenly shooting up. I knew this would happen, I always knew. For forty years I have avoided getting into a plane, I have stayed safely on the ground, never being higher than the upper deck of a bus, and now look at me. To make my family happy, to be able to accept the most amazing birthday present ever, I finally convince myself that all my fears are unfounded, I spend all that money on phobia treatment, I spend hours on the web finding out just how safe I will be, and here I am in the middle of the ocean with a rubbish lifejacket, a headache and a desire to throw up that is increasingly difficult to ignore.

Something bumps into my shoulder and I shriek. Dan would probably say I squealed like a girlie. Images of dead bodies or, worse still, parts of dead bodies, populate my mind. I turn my head slowly and am so relieved to make out the form of a canvas holdall, with luggage label attached, that I burst into tears. The holdall is huge – the sort of thing that, in other circumstances, I might have joked about using to transport a dead body. I reach my arms over the top of it and for a few minutes I lie there, not really awake but not quite asleep, tears mingling with the salt water lapping around my face. This is better than the lifejacket. It's more solid and more buoyant.

Not for long. I am almost dozing when I realise that my new liferaft is gradually absorbing water and is sinking. When I first grabbed onto it, my shoulders and most of my back were out of the water, with my head hanging over the edge, face just above the water. Now, I am holding my head up to keep it out of the water, and, although I am still lying across the bag, my head is the only part of me not under water. I let it go.

It's dark now, but there's a moon and stars above me and I can see that other pieces of luggage are bobbing about on the waves. Many of them are sinking slowly, as they absorb water.

There are a couple of enormous suitcases, made of that rigid plastic. One is pink, with flowers on it and the other is a really cool design, made to look like a washing machine. It's mainly white, with a circular picture of the door in the centre, and a couple of fake buttons at the top for switching it on and off. I saw one like this, when I was shopping for my own luggage, but it was far too expensive for me. Both these cases are floating really well. I swim slowly towards the washing machine and try to grab onto it. I slide off and my head goes under the water again. When I surface, I throw up. I am so tired. I need to sleep and I need painkillers. I wash my mouth out with sea-water and try a different approach. The suitcase has two handles, one at the top and one on one of the long sides. This time, I move round to the long side of the suitcase, on the opposite side from the handle. I place both hands gently on the top of the case and allow my legs to sink so that I am almost standing up next to the case. I fiddle around with one hand until I have pulled my dress up and tucked it into my knickers, to keep it out of the way. That takes ages and I let go of the suitcase a couple of times but I am determined. I have a sort of plan and I think that, if it doesn't work, I will not have the energy to try again. Perhaps that will be okay. All I want right now is to fall asleep. I wonder vaguely whether, if you start to drown when you're asleep, you wake up.

I take a deep breath, allow myself to sink further, until the water laps over my closed lips, then I kick upwards, really hard, with my legs, and throw the top of my body over the suitcase, reaching out desperately with both hands.

I can't find the handle, my hands are sliding back and I am ready to give up. Then it's there. I have grasped it with my right hand and I slowly pull my left arm over and now I am clutching the handle with both hands, and my body is resting across the case, head hanging over my hands, legs trailing behind. I relax. Now I will find out just how buoyant this suitcase really is, with my added weight.

I must have started to doze again, because I jerk into life as my hands are releasing the handle and I am sliding backwards. I'm just in time, grabbing onto the handle again and pulling myself more firmly onto my life-raft. My head hurts so badly and I need to throw up again. This is not going to work unless I can find a way to fix myself on. I can't stay awake much longer. Something in my head tells me that I obviously have a concussion and you're not supposed to sleep if you're concussed, but I am beyond caring; I need to sleep. On the other hand, I have just enough energy left to know that I don't want to die.

There are only two more pieces of luggage left. All the rest have sunk or floated away. The pink flowery suitcase is closest, but beyond that there's a black one, with a rainbow luggage strap around it. So that's the one I aim for, sculling clumsily with one hand and my feet. There's a rhythm to the waves and once I tune in to it, although I go round in circles a lot, I gradually make progress towards my target. It's painfully slow, and a couple of times I have to stop and close my eyes because my vision is so blurred that I can't separate the suitcase from the waves. I throw up twice, getting most of it into the sea, but my arms are now sticky and my long hair is lumpy from when I rested my head briefly to wait for a bout of dizziness to pass.

I struggle to grab the other suitcase, fumble around to undo the strap without actually unthreading it from the way it's wrapped through the handles and then wrap it around myself and clip it closed again. My original liferaft has floated away, but I feel a little more secure with this one. It took weeks to do this and when I was finally tied to the suitcase I have no recollection of being pleased or relieved. I just let go and allowed myself to be rocked to sleep.

ii

My legs are on fire. Flames are licking around the backs of my knees and ankles. I am being tortured. The left side of my face has been glued to a sheet of sandpaper and my eyelids have been sewn shut.

My hands are not tied though, and I gradually slide the right one up to my face, exploring carefully. By placing my first finger above my right eye and the thumb below, and gently pulling the lashes apart, I discover that my eye will open.

I am not being tortured, I am lying on a beach. The left side of my face is pressed into the sand and, when I lift my head, half the beach remains firmly attached to it. I am awake. There is no part of me that doesn't hurt, but the pain in the backs of my legs is the worst.

I start to sit up, needing to know what has happened to my legs. My head spins, pain lancing through it, and I fall back to the sand.

I am awake again, eyes firmly closed. This time, I take things more carefully. I bring both hands up under my chest and very, very slowly, push myself up into a sitting position. There is sand all over my face and, as I move, I feel it scraping my skin. The pain in the back of my legs is worse when I bend them, but it's the only way to sit up. I can feel the sun beating down on me, but I can't see anything. I bring my hands up to my face and prise apart my eyelids, squinting against the brightness. Gradually my eyes accustom themselves to being open and I take in my surroundings.

There's a vast expanse of blue, blue sky above me. There are no clouds, just this amazing sun, and somewhere in my brain I understand that the pain in the back of my legs is a very serious sunburn. I shield my eyes with my hands, to shut out some of the light, and I see that they are covered in sand and small clumps of something pale and lumpy.

I am on a beach. Not the kind with deckchairs and umbrellas and ice-cold margaritas. There are no running, laughing children, no sandcastles, no smell of sun-tan lotion. There is no-one splashing around in the water, there are no inflatable toys, no pedalos, no-one is playing volleyball. There is nothing here that I recognise, except sand and sea. And a few rocks. And the smell of vomit.

My headache persists, but it's at a lower level now and I don't feel dizzy any more. My vision seems to be ok; the blurring has gone. My brain is beginning to engage. I understand that the lumps in the sand were created by me throwing up. I am grateful that I washed up face down, because otherwise I would probably have choked and died, without knowing anything about it.

I struggle to my feet and turn, very slowly, in a circle. There's the sea and there's sand and there are rocks and, several yards behind me, there are trees and shrubs. I couldn't name any of them, but then again, I couldn't name the trees and shrubs in my own garden. The sea stretches a million miles into the distance, uninterrupted. Under other circumstances, I would think it beautiful. The beach sweeps away from me in either direction, broken up only by small outcroppings of rocks.

Behind and above the trees, some distance away, I can see a rock-face. There are no people here, but that doesn't mean there are none close by. Perhaps I'm on someone's private beach -- private island, even. If I can find a way up there, perhaps at the top of the rock-face, there will be houses, people, civilisation.

But before I think about climbing or exploring, there are more pressing things to deal with. I am becoming more aware of my body; I stink of vomit, the pain in my legs is incredible and my throat is parched. I am aware of a thirst beyond anything I have ever experienced. To make matters worse, my right arm is throbbing and, when I look at it, I see a long gash, from just below my shoulder, to my elbow. The blood has dried and crusted, possibly assisted by the sand that's mixed in with it. I must have been here for a while, then. I am filthy and smelly and desperate for something to drink. In spite of my thirst, I want to try and clean myself up, at least a little, before I go looking for water. I need to take my clothes off. I struggle out of the lifejacket, thinking again about how useless it was.

And now I know why. The bright orange flash that I saw beneath the seat on the plane wasn't a lifejacket, it was a child's rucksack. In my confused state, with blurred vision and a brain that had just been bashed against a wall, I saw the colour and latched onto it. No wonder I had such trouble getting it on, and, of course, that there was no whistle, no light, no tapes with which to fasten it securely.

Pulling my cotton dress off, I move to the edge of the water and sit down, then gently shuffle forward, still sitting, until the water is lapping around my waist. It takes a long time to rinse the sand and blood from my skin. The sunburn on my legs and the gash on my arm sting fiercely, but I need to be clean. When I have finished with my body and my face, I slide further into the sea, until I am completely submerged, and start to work my fingers through my tangled hair, gradually removing as much of the sand and vomit as I can, surfacing only to take in air and then submerge myself again. When I'm done, I move back until I'm sitting on the sand with my feet in the water again.

The beach slopes gently away and the water is so clear. I can see fish, some tiny, in groups, and others larger, more solitary, swimming around my toes and further away. Beautiful colours. I want to paint them, but that's probably not the most important thing to be thinking about right now and anyway, what would I paint them *with*? Get a grip. Water, that's what I need first.

As I stand up, the pain at the back of my knees makes me cry out, but all that escapes my cracked lips is a hoarse grunt. I really do need to drink something soon.

I look out to sea, and then turn back to the sand and the trees. There is something wrong with this picture and now I know what it is. I have read the books, seen the movies, this is *not* how it happens. Where is the conveniently wrecked ship, just off-shore, containing all the materials and tools I will need to build a shelter, all the canned foods and barrels of fresh water that will sustain me, sailcloth to make clothes from, flares to attract a rescuer, possibly even a few chickens or a goat? Definitely an axe.

Failing that, where is the FedEx box, with the basketball that will become my best friend? Why, when I boarded the plane, was I not carrying a pen-knife with four million tiny tools, ideal for an occasion like this? Why wasn't I at least wearing sturdy lace-up shoes so that I could use the laces for something practical? Someone has messed up the script and I'm the one paying for it.

I take stock. I have the following items:

a child's rucksack
a pair of knickers
a bra
a cotton frock with a zip down the back

My sandals are gone. I was dressed for a holiday in Crete, not life on an island.

I sit down next to the rucksack and pull open the zip. There's stuff in here, and I tip it out. Now my list of belongings has grown to include:

an extremely soggy scrapbook, covered with clear plastic that's coming away now, with "Wh t l d   on y ho d ys" just about discernible on the cover some kind of hand-held computer game, with the word Nintendo on it. I doubt it's solar-powered

two books by Jacqueline Wilson, soggier even than the scrapbook

a packet of Skittles, surprisingly still intact. The wrapper is some sort of plastic, and I find myself wondering about how recyclable it is. It's easy to focus on irrelevancies.

a squashed chocolate mini-roll, the wrapper torn and the mini-roll soggy and flat

two small cartons of blackcurrant-flavoured drink, soggy but intact

a child's word puzzle book, soggy beyond redemption

five coloured pencils, red green, blue, yellow and purple, and a normal one

a green plastic hairband, with a small plastic flower attached

a small metal pencil sharpener

an eraser

an extremely soggy blue rabbit with one ear, that may once have been fluffy and cuddly

I imagine the child who carried this bag onto the plane, on her way to an exciting holiday in the sun. I see her in jeans and a green t-shirt, bright orange rucksack slung over one shoulder, dark hair loose down her back. Did I really see her when we were boarding, or is this all in my head? Where is she now? Was hers one of the twinkling lights I saw in the sea? Were her parents with her? Brothers and sisters?

And then my brain kicks in and I understand that right here, in front of me, is exactly what I need. Well, not exactly. Let's face it, sugary blackcurrant drink would not have been at the top of my list but, *oh my god,* there is a drink in my hand.

The straw is no longer attached to the carton, and I can't find it in the rucksack. I need to open the carton without losing any of its precious contents. I don't have a long, thin implement with which to pierce the tiny spot where the straw should go and I'm terrified of just trying to tear open the top and perhaps spilling my treasure out onto the sand. I force myself to work slowly, gradually tearing away a small corner of the carton, which is actually easy to do, because it has become soft and soggy with immersion.

I have made a hole and now I put my mouth over it completely before slowly tipping the carton to allow the contents to begin to trickle into my mouth. I only allow a small amount to cross my tongue before tipping the carton back to its upright position and then swilling the liquid around my mouth and swallowing.

It tastes disgusting. The carton may not have punctured, but it clearly allowed salt-water in somehow. The word osmosis comes to mind, but I don't know where from. Sugary, salty, thick blackcurrant liquid washes around my mouth and then down my throat. I was right to be careful. The first swallow is so painful that I start to cough, which makes the pain worse; and all the time, I am holding the carton away from myself and upright, desperate not to spill it while I'm shaking with the cough.

Once the coughing has stopped, I gradually drink more, in very small amounts, until half the carton has gone. Or half remains. I think that once I would have said I'm a "glass half full" sort of person, but now I'm not so sure.

I so want to drink all of it. After all, there is another carton. I won't though, because after that, what? I have no idea whether there is fresh water here, or whether I will even need it. What if, when I walk round past my current line of sight, I find a beach full of sunbathing holiday-makers, a hotel with a pool-side bar, a little girl in jeans and green t-shirt, happy to see her rucksack heading towards her? Ok, for now, perhaps I am glass half full.

I want to walk along the beach and check for signs of civilisation, but I don't want to just leave all my precious supplies here. God knows why, it's not as though someone's likely to come along and steal them, but I don't know whether the tide will come in, or an animal might come foraging. What kinds of animals are wild in Greece? This must *be* a Greek island, I think. I researched a lot of stuff about flying, and about the resort, but it never occurred to me that I might need to know about wild animals or, for that matter, wild plants. What's edible, what's going to kill me, or give me a horrendous rash.

My legs hurt so much, but at least my long hair seems to have protected the back of my neck. My arms are ok too, the left one was tucked underneath me and there was so much sand and vomit plastered to my right arm that it appears to have blocked the sun's rays.

Ok, be sensible. None of these things will be important to me if there are other people here, so it won't matter if they are taken. And, if there's no-one else here, my precious hoard is safe.

I lay all the books out so that they can begin to dry. I pull the zip on the rucksack all the way open and spread it as well as I can on the sand so that that too will dry.

Everything else just lies there on the sand. Looking at the pencils, I realise that I could have pierced the little silver spot in the top of the juice carton easily with one of them. My brain is woolly and I am scared. This is hard enough but, if I can't think, if my brain is damaged, what then? I pick up my dress, shake off as much sand as possible, and put it on. I don't bother to zip it up. I pick up the Skittles and the full carton of juice and then, very carefully, the half empty one. I'm not leaving food and drink behind.

Through all of this, the pain in my legs is constant and movement makes it worse. I realise I have been gritting my teeth so hard that my face aches. I force myself to relax the muscles but I still feel pain lancing across my forehead.

I'm ready to explore.

I walk very slowly. The skin on the backs of my legs, especially behind the knees, is so tight that every step sends pain shooting through them. I had thought that perhaps moving them would gradually make it better, but, if anything, it's worse. The sand is hot too, sometimes so hot that I find myself inadvertently speeding up, just because I have to keep lifting my feet.

In spite of the evidence all around me, in my head I have a picture of a cartoon island, small and round, with a solitary palm tree in the centre. On the map, Greek islands are tiny dots and many of them are apparently not even large enough to warrant a dot. And yet, wherever I am, this is much bigger than my mental image. So I am hopeful. As I trudge along the beach, I am more and more certain that this is not some tiny, uninhabited island. It is at least one of the smaller named ones, perhaps even the Greek mainland. Any minute now, I will hear voices, see a fence or a shed, indications of human interference with the landscape. A boat would do. Anything that tells me there are people somewhere close. A dog or cat would be even better although I know a lot of those are just left to roam wild, but at least they would be an indication that I m not alone. I'm sure I read somewhere that there are bears in Greece. Wildcats and wolves, too. I did my homework, rummaged through the internet, but I didn't pay huge amounts of attention to the results. I was more concerned with the flight. There are tortoises as well, and all sorts of lizards, which I looked forward to seeing. Perhaps I imagined the bears? Let's not think about that right now. One thing at a time. First, I need to look for people and, if I can't find any, I need to look for water.

The sun is burning down and for a while I try moving closer to the trees, looking for shade, but the ones nearest the beach are scrubby and prickly, and some of the roots extend across the sand, tripping me. There are some stunted, dark, pine trees and the undergrowth holds needles, sharp against my bare feet. So now, I am walking about half-way between the sea and the trees, and my head is aching. I want a hat. The last thing I need is sun-stroke, or more sunburn. I consider taking off my dress and draping it over my head, but that would be tantamount to acknowledging that I won't find any people here. Not ready for that.

I'm not sure how far I have walked, and it has felt like a straight line, but when I turn to look back, I can't see the rucksack any more and I realise that I have walked round a curve so gentle that I didn't notice it at all. Also, far from forming a straight track, my footprints meander in gentle curves towards the trees, then back towards the sea, then straight for a few metres, then off again.

To my right, there's a small group of rocks, half in and half out of the water. Geckos are sunbathing on some of them, apparently unbothered by my presence. I assume they're geckos, they are definitely lizards of some sort. Beautiful green with light brown markings, frozen in place, no hint of movement, until I walk across to sit on the flattest rock, and the geckos dart away, then settle again at a distance from me, once more turned to stone.

I flap my feet about in a small pool, staring out across the water. I thought the rock would be cool against the back of my legs, but of course it's hot, so, after a few minutes, I slide down and sit in the water. It feels wonderful on the backs of my legs.

Again, I see the fish, dozens of tiny, silver, darting ones and a few larger, slower and further away. Ellie would love
Ellie would

Oh my god. How long have I been here? Several hours at least, possibly longer. And before that, in the plane and in the water. I have never once thought about them, the people I love, the people who probably believe I am dead, lost to them forever. I have thought about sunburn and thirst and fish and bears and geckos, but not once have I considered Ellie and Dan. Caitlin, Sam.

News of the plane crash must have been on TV. Whether or not others survived, my name will not be on any list, not even on the list of dead bodies recovered. What are they thinking? Are there sharks in these waters? Do they imagine me ripped to pieces and eaten? Slowly falling asleep in the water and drowning? Blown to shreds in mid-air? Resting on the sea-bed in the carcass of the plane? How did they hear about it? If today is the day after the flight, then it's Saturday. Ellie's always up early at the weekend, wanting to make the most of every free minute, but she doesn't watch the news. She says she can pick up anything of interest from Facebook. Dan doesn't leave his room on a Saturday until hunger drives him down to maraud through the fridge. So, with luck, Caitlin or Sam has heard something, seen something, and will find a way to tell them. Oh god, the first time I have been away from them for more than one night and this happens. They worked hard to convince me that they would cope alone and were both pretty grumpy when I insisted that Caitlin and Sam would be staying over while I was away. Apparently, nearly seventeen is easily old enough to be totally self-sufficient. They would both get themselves up and out for school when term started again, two days before I was due home; of course they would eat sensibly, how dare I think they would have wild parties, not finish their holiday homework assignments, leave all the dishes and laundry for me to deal with when I came back?

If I go back. What are they thinking now, my babies? Do they think they're alone, that I am dead; drowned or eaten or blown up? And Caitlin, my baby sister. She, of course, is a proper grown-up, not a teenager, but I have always been there for her, we have supported one another, never lived more than a mile apart, except when she was away at uni. And Sam. Not just Caitlin's partner but a real member of our family now, for seven years. I suppose, as Caitlin and I lost our parents so long ago, and Sam's are refusing to have anything to do with her since she told them about her relationship, we all understand how important the family we do have is. We take care of one another. And now I'm gone. What if I never get home? Never see my babies grow up? I won't see Ellie get her black belt next month, I won't know whether Dan wins the history prize he's worked so hard for.

My face is wet. I realise that I am crying but only a few tears run down my cheeks. I need to stop, I can't afford to lose the moisture. I'm so, so sad, but I must not cry if I want to survive, to go home to my babies. I wipe my face with the back of my hand and then lick my hand. A few deep breaths help to balance me, and then I look up and see that I have been sitting here much longer than I thought. The sun is quite low in the sky now and, although it's still very warm, the heat is much more gentle. I'm not sure what to do. My head is throbbing and I just want to sit here and cry, but I pull up a picture of my twins and tell myself to get a grip; focus. I won't get home to them by sitting here feeling sorry for myself.

Slowly, I drink the remainder of the open carton of juice. I am very thirsty but so far, although it's hard to remember when I last ate, I'm not hungry at all. I can't bring myself to leave the empty carton here. It's not just my aversion to littering, but I have no way of knowing whether an empty juice carton might be exactly what saves my life at some point.

I'm undecided now. Should I keep walking, and, if so, for how long? If this is an island, surely I will eventually end up back at the rucksack and books, my treasure hoard? If it's not an island, I won't need them, so it won't matter if I never see them again. But what if it's an enormous island, far bigger than I have been imagining? What if it takes days to get all the way round?

I can't make a decision. Without thinking about it, I put down the juice cartons, one empty and one full, and the packet of Skittles, and, still wearing my dress, I walk out into the sea and allow myself to float gently on my back on the lapping waves, facing towards the shore. The sand slopes very gently into the sea and, if I want to, I can put my feet down and stand, up to my waist in water. I float for a while, just letting go, feeling the soothing water on my burning legs, eyes closed. I soothe my aching head by dipping it backwards and allowing the water to gently lap across my face.

Eventually, I stand up, facing the beach, water streaming from me, and open my eyes. And then I see it. At this distance from the shore, although only a few feet out, I have a better view of what's ahead of me, further round the gently curving beach. In perhaps another fifty metres, the beach comes to an abrupt end at what appears to be a sheer cliff wall that extends out into the sea and then gradually tapers downwards until, about fifty feet out, it's just another pile of rocks. So much for finding a holiday resort, a farm, a lone walker. There is no-one here, no-one to save me.

I'm tired and I want to sleep. I walk out of the water and my wet dress clings to me, tightening around my knees and nearly tripping me. I should have taken it off and I don't know why I didn't. Did I really think someone was going to come wandering along the beach and see me swimming in my underwear? And would it have mattered if they did? I manage, with some difficulty, to take it off, and I walk slowly towards the cliff face, dragging the dress along the sand and carrying my meagre supplies in the other hand.

At the base of the cliff there are rocks, creating small, sandy areas like oddly-shaped roofless rooms. I drape my wet, sandy dress over one of the rocks, carefully place the Skittles and juice against the cliff-face, and curl up on the sand.

I wake with a hoarse shriek. Something small, with a lot of legs, was running over my body. Instinctively, I have leapt up, causing flashes of pain down my legs and through my head, and am standing in the moonlight, in my underwear, frantically trying to see what it was. It's gone, of course, and I have no idea what it was. Also, I'm cold. The sun set some time ago, judging by the height of the moon in the sky, and I have been lying on a cold beach in my bra and knickers. I'm shivering so much that my teeth start to chatter. I didn't even think that was a real thing; thought it was just a figure of speech. It's not. I need fire, but I don't think rubbing a packet of skittles on an empty juice carton will work.

My dress is dry, so I put it on, but that doesn't really help and I'm still cold. I know I won't be able to sleep again unless I can get warm, but what am I supposed to do? The stars are amazing and the moon is bright, but it's really dark down here, and I trip over a rock as I struggle to find my way out of the maze of little "rooms" and onto the main beach. Once there, I decide that the best way to keep warm will be to walk, so I start trying to walk back towards my treasure hoard. It's not easy. I think I'm walking in a straight line, but twice I find myself walking on pine needles. I'm making very slow progress and not really feeling any warmer.

The sea is so quiet, I imagine that it's not there at all, that some huge monster has sucked it all back, leaving my island connected to the rest of the world by a vast stretch of sand. I can walk home. That only lasts until I wander blindly into the water. Even now, when the air is cold, the water feels warm though, so for a while I use the water's edge as a guide, walking with one foot in the water and one on the sand and I'm moving more quickly. I'm a little warmer now, and using the sea as a guide has relaxed me, made me less worried about tripping, so I am walking at a normal pace, with purpose.

When I trip and land with my face in the water and my shin scraped against the rock, my scream of anger comes out as a hoarse croak. Fuck, fuck, fuck. How did I forget about the bloody rocks? I spent long enough sitting on them feeling sorry for myself. My throat hurts from trying to yell and that, of course, is when I realise I forgot to pick up the Skittles and the second juice carton when I set off, so I can't even soothe my throat with a drink. Oh god, I am so useless. How on earth do I expect to survive here? I am so very much not the right person to be in this situation. I know nothing about survival skills, and my brain feels like mush anyway.

I sit up and reach out towards the rock that tripped me. I need to know where it is before I try and regain my feet.

This isn't a rock, it's a uniform shape. Plastic? My despair forgotten, I'm trying hard not to be excited as I run my hands carefully over my find. But yes, I'm right, it's a suitcase. A big one, and it's still in one piece and closed.

Aha! This is my boat full of supplies, my axe and goats and chickens. This is my hoard of canned foods and bottled water. This is my rescue plane, my liferaft. Perhaps the books and movies are right, after all.

Ok, so probably not a goat. Definitely not chickens. Equally certainly, there will be no canned food and no liferaft. But surely, in this suitcase, there must be something I can use. Clothes; at least I can be warmer. I am sitting on the sand, wet through and shivering, clutching the handle of the suitcase and thinking about my own case. What did I pack into it? Swimsuits, lightweight cotton trousers, jeans, t shirts, three cotton dresses, sandals, flip-fops, one pair of nice shoes, knickers, bras, a huge beach towel, adapters, so I would be able to charge my phone and use the travel iron and hairdryer that Ellie insisted I take with me. Make-up, nail-clippers, shower gel, toothbrush, hairbrush, toothpaste, shampoo and sun-screen, books. Teabags, my favourite coffee bags. And of course, my paints and brushes. Nothing that I could build a shelter with, nothing to start a fire with. But who knows what might be in this suitcase? Anything is possible.

It's too dark to do anything now, and I'm so cold that I can hardly feel my hands. My euphoria wanes. Slowly, stopping every few feet, I drag the suitcase back towards the rock rooms and, when I get there, I drop the suitcase, scramble over the rocks, whining as I scrape my shins yet again, and fumble around until I find my juice. It's nearly impossible to open it with my freezing fingers, but I get there. Then, very carefully, I hold the carton to my lips and drink it. All of it. What's the point of saving it? If I don't find water tomorrow, I'm probably going to die here anyway, however many woolly jumpers I find in the suitcase.

I sit down, lean my back against a rock, knees pulled up to my chest, in spite of the pain from the sunburn, hug myself to try and keep out the cold, and wait for the sun to come up.

iv

In spite of the cold, I must have slept, because the next thing I am aware of is the warmth of the sun on my limbs and the fact that my whole body is itching. My dress is dry now but there's so much sand in it, from where I dragged it along the beach yesterday, that it's rubbing against my skin like sandpaper.

I slowly stretch my arms out and then up, reaching for the blue sky and wriggling my shoulders to loosen them. I straighten my cramped legs, wincing against the pain behind my knees, and stretch out my toes, and then I scramble to my feet and look down at myself.

My dress is filthy, encrusted with sand and salt. My legs are scraped and bruised. On the plus side, the long gash in my right arm seems to be healing well already and doesn't look swollen or infected, perhaps thanks to the time I spent in the sea yesterday. The backs of my legs still burn and there are blisters forming behind my knees. I run my fingers gently up the back of my legs to the top of my thighs and wince, even at this light touch. As I wonder what my face looks like, I flash back again, for a fraction of a second, to an image of blood and glass. It's gone before I can catch hold of it, but I lift my right hand to my face and gently explore. Above my right eye is a large, sticky lump, sensitive to the light touch of my fingertips. I flash back again and, this time, I hold onto the image for a second longer. It's not glass, it's that stuff they use for mirrors in the toilets on trains and planes. There's a smear of blood on it. I can't see any more, but I don't think I need to. I remember. I remember going into the toilet; I took my handbag with me, so I could check my make-up after I peed. I remember peeing. I remember standing up and turning to the mirror, balancing my bag on the tiny sink so that I could open it. That's all. And then I was looking for a life-jacket. There's no need to fill in the gaps.

Enough. Right now, I am here and alive. Not in great shape, but it could be so very much worse. I give myself a mental shake and continue checking out the state of my body.

I lift my dress and see rough, red patches of skin on my stomach and thighs, where the sand has abraded them. If I am going to be here for more than a few days, I need to take better care of myself physically.

I take the dress off and drop it on the sand. There must be clean clothes in the suitcase, which is lying a few feet away, and that's a start.

But right now I need a drink. Now, I wish I had had more control last night. I am so thirsty, but there's nothing left. Last night, I behaved like a spoiled child and now I'm suffering for it. I need to find water. Should I head back up the beach and walk on in the other direction? Should I try walking into the trees? Whatever I do, I need to take the suitcase with me, I don't want to be separated from it, but it's heavy and my legs hurt. I could boil sea-water and then condense it, to make fresh water. If I had something to make fire with, and a kettle or saucepan and a plate to hold above it, to catch the steam and turn it back into water. Yeah, sure, and I could make a raft out of the rucksack and a couple of pencils, while I'm at it.

I'm standing with my back to the sun, facing the cliff. I rub my eyes, carefully avoiding the lump above the right one. Something's wrong with them, the cliff face seems to be moving, blurring, the surface is rippling and my head hurts from the effort of trying to make it keep still. Oh god, what's wrong with me? I'm going mad, or maybe blind.

I rub my eyes again and again, but the rock still ripples in the sunlight, as though it's alive. I imagine a swarm of tiny, rock-coloured insects streaming down the cliff towards me. I take a step closer, nervous, but needing to know. And then I laugh out loud. The sounds comes from my mouth like a hideous cackle, and my throat grates, but I don't care. I step right up to the cliff face and lean into it, tongue out, to lap at the gentle stream of water running diagonally across and down. It's about eighteen inches across at the widest point and maybe six at the narrowest. A tiny, trickling waterfall, following the cracks and folds in the surface of the rock face. Somewhere, at the top of the cliff, there's a stream or a pond or something, and it's leaking over the edge and following a crack, a trail, down to the sea. I can see now that, at the base, the sand is wet, but it's not obvious unless I am right on top of it, because of the scattered rocks all around this area.

I could have walked away and headed off in the other direction. I might have walked in among the trees and lost myself. I was standing right next to the most precious thing in the world and I nearly missed it. My mood swings up again.

After a few mouthfuls, I force myself to stop. My stomach hurts and I know I need to be careful. Then panic overtakes me. I have no idea whether this water source is always there or whether something has happened at the top of my world to cause an overflow that could dry up at any time. Perhaps I didn't see it yesterday, because it wasn't there. I fill both my juice cartons and place them against a rock, away from the sun. I wish I had a bucket, ten buckets, a hundred.

I don't have a bucket and I need to get a grip. Somewhere in my mind, I can see that every small thing that happens is having a disproportionate impact on my emotions. The good things make me laugh aloud and feel like singing. The bad reduce me to instant despair, or blazing anger. I lap some more water from the rock-face, take a deep breath and sit down on the sand.

I need to think, to plan and to try and be rational. I have always been a list-maker, I need to make one now. I need to stop just doing one thing after another and organise myself.

Ok, water. That's number one and I have it now. That means I will stay alive, at least for several days. Water is much more important than food. So, this place, with the rock rooms and the water, this is where I need to keep coming back to. I'm not ready to think about making some kind of proper base because I still don't know whether, if I walk in the other direction, I might find people. I'm not completely sure that this is an uninhabited island, I'm still holding on to a hope that I'm just in an isolated part of one of the big ones; perhaps I'm on Crete? I could be really close to the hotel I should have slept in last night, before heading off for my wonderful painting holiday. Right now, I should be sitting in the sun, brush in hand, a cool drink beside me, creating my masterpiece. I recall the coloured pencils and the scrapbook in the rucksack. I smile; perhaps I can still create something, but it won't be quite what I had envisaged.

Stop dreaming and make a list. I actually say this aloud to myself. I need to focus. So, if I am on an uninhabited island, walking in the other direction might take me to a proper stream, even (in my wildest dreams) an abandoned hut or something. But until I know, this will be my temporary home, the place I return to. Also, that will mean I don't need to drag the suitcase anywhere.

The next thing on my list is getting the suitcase open, because I need to be warmer at night and I may find things that will make the rest of the list easier. After that, it's food. There must be stuff growing here that I can eat. And fire would be nice. Funny really. It's not just because it would keep me warm at night; I think fire would provide a kind of comfort. Oh, and I want to go back and collect the rucksack and its contents; whatever I find in the suitcase, I shouldn't discount the things I already have. And then I need to explore in the other direction, and in the trees.

So…

Water – tick
Suitcase
Food

Fire
Rucksack
Explore

That's enough for now.

First, I will get the suitcase open and find out what's inside. I need clothes, both to protect myself from the sun and to keep me warm at night. And who knows what else I might find?

I couldn't see the suitcase last night, although I could tell that it was one of those rigid plastic ones. Now, I examine it carefully. It's red and green, a bit scratched up, but still in one piece. It is, of course, locked. There's a tiny hole in the tip of each of the zip-pulls and someone has linked a small padlock through them, to hold them together. It looks pretty feeble and I could probably lever it off with a screwdriver.

That makes me laugh again. I'm relieved to discover that my voice is sounding more normal, since I found the water.

Okay, so no screwdriver. I gaze around me and move closer to the trees, looking for something I can use. There are no loose stones or rocks, only the large ones, fixed in their places on the beach. As I move in among the trees, I find sticks and twigs, but nothing that looks strong enough to snap the padlock with. My mood slumps again. So much for being rational. Frustrated, I stomp around amongst the trees, not caring that I scrape and scratch my bare feet and the backs of my legs scream at me. The whole world is conspiring against me. Every time something goes right, something else is made impossible. I force myself to stop and take a deep breath.

It's cooler in here and it occurs to me for the first time that I do not have to be on the beach in the burning sun all the time. I probably wouldn't want to sleep in here because there must be small (I hope) animals, and lots of insects, but in the daytime, here among the trees, I am comfortable. And now, because I am calmer and not stomping around, I look at the tree immediately in front of me and can't believe what I'm seeing. Bananas. Small, but perfectly formed, there are several hands of them on the tree, the lower ones easily within reach. And, just like that, I'm starving. I reach up cautiously, with both hands, and detach a single banana with care. I am about to peel it when, just as suddenly, I am desperate to pee. It's the first time since I got here and I suppose I just didn't have enough fluid to waste until now. But now, with water sloshing around in my stomach and food in my hands, my body is coming back to life. I am hungry and I need to pee. I am alive.

I look around for somewhere to pee, that I won't step in afterwards, and decide on a fairly clear area at the base of the cliff, where the trees are farther apart and there's very little scrub. The ground this far in is no longer sand, it's rocky, with patches of soil that don't look as though they could sustain any kind of life, and yet the trees around me are proof that they do.

I am so civilised. Once I have peed, in spite of my hunger, I can't eat my banana until I have washed my hands, so I head back to the beach. I step out from the trees, close to the rocks I sat on yesterday, and there, in the distance, so small that I can hardly make them out I see boats – ships? What's the difference between a boat and a ship anyway? There are at least four, but they're so far away that I can't even make out colours, they are just blobs on the water. And something in the air. Must be a helicopter, because it doesn't seem to be moving at all. I know it's pointless, but I leap up and down, waving my arms and yelling at the top of my scratchy voice. Why haven't I got a blazing fire going, so that I can signal them with the smoke? I put my thumb and forefinger between my lips and generate the loudest, shrillest whistle I have ever managed. I do it again and again. It's a waste of time. When I finally give up, my legs are screaming at me from all the leaping about, and I have to walk into the water and just lie there to cool them. I don't cry. What's the point.

I sit on a rock and eat my banana, but all the pleasure I felt a few minutes ago, when I found it, has gone.

As I swallow the last bite, I feel slightly sick, so I sit very still and take several slow, deep breaths until it passes. Now, I am hungry again, but I should wait before I eat more. I'm about to bury the banana skin, so that it doesn't attract flies, when I decide to lay it on the rocks to dry out. I have no idea what I can use it for, but it seems foolish to waste anything right now. I walk slowly back to the suitcase.

If I can't attack the padlock with a rock, I will have to attack a rock with the padlock. I drag the case towards the nearest rock and slide the padlocked zip-pulls round until they are away from the suitcase handles and facing the rock. I move round behind the suitcase and grasp it with both hands and then shove it forward, hard, against the rock. Great. I have managed to scrape the suitcase and slightly bend one of the zip-pulls, but the padlock remains intact. I try again and again. The fourth time, my finger gets caught in the handle and I break a nail, ripping it off down to the fingertip. I scream and swear, then suck my finger for a few minutes, gazing out across the sea, in case someone's on their way to rescue me. Turns out they're not, so I have another go. The sixth or seventh time, I'm getting careless with frustration and I trip and fall forwards when I push the suitcase, bashing my left arm on the rock. It's not bleeding but there will be a massive bruise. I scream more abuse at the universe, which makes my headache even worse, and drag the suitcase upright to try again.

And, oh my god, look at that! It's not what I planned but it's success. The padlock remains intact, but one of the zip-pulls has snapped off so that, although it is still padlocked to the other one, it is no longer attached to the zip. I can open the case.

I don't though. I am exhausted and suddenly afraid. As long as I don't open the case, it can contain everything I need. Once I have looked inside it, I won't be able to not know, to forget what I see. The case could contain my goats and chickens or it could be full of children's clothes and toys, or business stuff – files and folders, samples, for a brief moment I see a suitcase full of cosmetics, then tiny vacuum cleaners and then one full of encyclopaedias. Too many old films, watched when I was younger.

I try hard not to think about the things I want most, but I can't help it. I know this is fantasy and I try hard to shake it from my head, which is aching badly, but there's a list. A crazy one, and if I stop to think too much I will start to worry about the bang on my head and the effect it's having on my mood and my thoughts. So, I don't stop to think about that, I allow myself to make a list.

box of waterproof matches
flare-gun
knife
scissors
shampoo
sleeping bag
toothbrush
paracetamol
toothpaste
saucepan
mobile phone
chocolate

I have written my list in the sand with a stick and now I make a small cross next to each of the impossible items. Then I rub the crosses out. Nothing is impossible until the case is open. I add chickens and a goat to my list, and then an axe. It's finished.

I must open the suitcase. I sit on the sand, in front of it and slowly slide the zips all the way to the back on either side. All I have to do is lift the lid. I know that the contents will be wet, because the zip is set into cloth, which must have allowed water in, but it's in one piece, so everything is still in there. Everything. All my dreams. My future.

Ok. Deep breath. Reach out with both hands and lift the lid about two inches. Scream and drop it, shuffling back across the sand, against the nearest rock, hands to my face, blocking out the world. My head is full of images of blood and glass and a brief flash of a face – my face – in the cracked mirror, blood running down across my cheek and over my lips. Orange. All I saw when I lifted the lid was bright orange. The colour of life-jackets, the colour of rucksacks.

It feels like hours before I am able to move forward and try again. To tell myself that there is a piece of orange clothing in the suitcase, perhaps a t-shirt, or a bright, Hawaiian-style shirt, remind myself that I am safe here, on the beach and not crawling through a sinking plane in search of a life-jacket.

It's not a life-jacket, it's an enormous, bright orange beach towel. Wet, but not soaking. I drape it over the nearest rocks to dry and continue working my way through the case.

v

Day three.

Have decided to keep a journal. First, I'll just recap how yesterday finished, to bring things up to date.

I took every item out of the suitcase and draped as much as possible over the rocks to dry in the sun. My mood swung up and down as I unpacked and, when I had finished, I was overwhelmed. I sat, surrounded by all this stuff, with no sense of what I should do next. I couldn't remember my plan and my carefully written wish-list in the sand was scuffed and illegible.

I stuck the baseball cap on my head and walked away from it all, back along the beach, towards the rucksack. Didn't even take my water carton with me. All the way, I was crying. The twins were in my thoughts constantly. I remembered their faces, their voices, first words, first school reports, screaming rows with Dan over the lies he told about his homework, how hard it was to stand back and not interfere when Ellie fell out with her best friend. I wondered how they were and what they were thinking? Did they feel guilty for planning this amazing fortieth birthday surprise with Caitlin and Sam. Did Caitlin and Sam feel guilty? Did they all think I was dead? Will they ever know what happened to me?

I had no tissues, nothing to blow my nose on. Twice, I walked into the water to wash my face, rinsing away the tears and snot. I tried to imagine what my face looked like, and was glad I couldn't see it.

When I reached the rucksack, everything lay exactly as I had left it. The rucksack and the blue rabbit were dry. The Jacqueline Wilson books were dry too, but many of the pages were stuck together. It's not really my kind of thing anyway, it's for kids, I would be more likely to use the pages to start a fire. If I had matches. I think I was disappointed to find everything still there; if things had disappeared, I would have known I was not alone.

The scrapbook was dry and I was able to separate most of the pages quite easily, perhaps because they are much thicker than the pages in the books. The pages, originally all different colours, were now all swirls of beautiful mixed colour. My mind was almost blank, I wasn't really thinking at all. I picked up the red pencil and carefully completed the original title on the front of the scrapbook. Now it very clearly says "What I did on my holidays". And then, I opened it and started to write.

I wrote for a long time, allowing myself to go back into the last few days and experience them all over again, as I described them. I cried a lot, but there was something cathartic in getting it all out and onto the first few pages of the scrapbook. By the time I had reached the part where I opened the suitcase though, my writing had shrunk to the smallest I could manage, squashed up tight, as I began to come out of my daze and start thinking about reality. About the fact that this paper is all there is in the world, and if I intend to keep a journal, I must take care to use it well.

So, from now on, it's a journal. Only important stuff will be recorded. Today's entry will probably be the longest.

I brought the rucksack and it's contents back to my base. I felt that it was important to list the contents of the suitcase, but didn't want to waste paper from the scrapbook, so I tore out the first few pages from something called "My sister Jodie" – the ones with the title and publication date and lots of empty space -- and wrote the list on them.

Giant orange beach towel
Giant blue beach towel
Seven brand new M&S t-shirts in various colours, all with the labels still on, all XXL
Ten pairs of XXL boxer shorts, mostly checked or striped, none of them new

Four pairs of black socks

Three pairs of shorts, all light brown, all XXL

Two enormous pairs of jeans

Two huge pairs of swimming shorts, with that weird mesh lining that men's swimshorts sometimes have

A lightweight, blue cotton jacket, XXL

A red baseball cap with "Red Sox" on the peak, in black

A plastic wash-bag containing toothpaste, toothbrush (not new), shower gel, shampoo, factor 20 sun-screen, nail scissors and hair gel

A packet of three disposable plastic razors

Two adaptors for plugging things in in Europe

A phone charging lead

A travel iron

A packet of sixteen paracetamol. The cardboard outer soggy and falling apart, but the plastic bit that you pop the pills out of is fine

A pair of reading glasses, brand new and still with the little tag that says they are 3.5, whatever that means. Will I grow so old here that I will need them?

Two books by James Patterson; Kiss the Girls and Along Came a Spider. One by Steven King; Rose Madder. I've never read any of their stuff before, I'm more of a historical fiction sort of person. I like the idea of a book called Rose Madder though; it's a lovely colour.

A swim mask and snorkel

A plastic comb

A pair of size 11 sandals

A pair of huge flip-flops

One blue M&S shirt, brand new, with the labels still on. Presumably in case the owner went "somewhere nice" one evening.

When I'd finished writing the list I was in tears again. Ok, yes, I did want clothes. But not these. I don't know what I had imagined, but I now have a feeling, in spite of the heat here, that fluffy pyjamas might have been involved. And definitely food. Of course, I will use these things as well as I can, but this is not what I was hoping for.

The snorkel is exciting. I've never used one before, but it can't be difficult. Not much practical use, as far as I can tell, but fun.

The washing stuff and sunscreen and scissors are great. My mouth tastes disgusting from all the throwing up, in spite of the drinks of juice and water. Couldn't wait to clean my teeth. Who cares that someone else has used the toothbrush before me? That's the least of my worries.

I have an idea that the disposable razors can be useful, but nothing specific comes to mind.

The paracetamols are like gold. The one very clear thing I wanted that has been provided.

The adaptors and travel iron made me cry.

The flip-flops and sandals are huge and I fell over when I tried to walk in them. Might find a use for them, though.

Books. If I'm here for a long time, they will be my only company. I imagined myself reaching a point where I can recite them, word for word, the way Will Smith does with the Shrek movie in I am Legend. Started crying again.

No matches, flares, chickens or goats. No magic fire-making equipment. Nothing to build a shelter with. No axe. No mobile phone.

The sun is setting. I will wrap myself in a beach towel and sleep. I'll feel better tomorrow

Day four

Bit stiff when I woke up, but not too cold. Will make a pillow from some of the clothes this evening. Bananas and water for breakfast. And one paracetamol. There are fifteen left.

Removed my crunchy, salty bra and knickers. Walked into the sea and washed as well as I could manage, including very carefully trying to clean up the lump on my forehead, using a pair of boxer sorts. I used the shower gel. I don't think this tiny bit of pollution will cause the end of the world. How quickly our priorities change.

Dried myself, then laid the towel and boxer shorts out to dry. Scrubbed out my bra and knickers as well as I could in the sea, then rinsed them in the fresh water from the rock face and laid them out to dry. Smothered myself in sunscreen. Not on the backs of my legs though, I think it's too late for that, I'll just keep on with the salt-water. Chose a green t-shirt to wear, belted it with the phone charger lead, put on the hat, took some water in a juice carton, and walked all the way to the other end of the beach. The t-shirt is huge and kept falling off my shoulders but I don't feel right just wearing nothing. Walking was still very painful, so I stopped often to give my legs a break. Each time, I walked into to the water and sat for a few minutes, to allow the salt-water to sooth the burns. I really think this is worse than normal sunburn. I can't bear to touch the skin behind my knees at all, and even if I had trousers that fitted, I couldn't possibly wear them.

The beach ends in much the same way as "my" end, with the rock face, although the beach is wider there and the rocks don't go so far out into the sea. There's another narrow waterfall, but it's a bit further back from the sea and ends in a small pool that trickles across the sand to the sea. Drank my water and refilled the carton. Headache slightly better.

Saw an aeroplane. Tiny, silver piece of magic, a million miles above me. Zero chance that they saw me. Cried.

Removed all my clothes and walked out into the water, swimming until I could see past the rock face. Still hoping for people, noise, something, anything. No. There's an almost sheer rock face, as far as I can see. It's as though a giant rock was thrown into the sea and then someone came along and carved out a tiny section on one side, just so I would have somewhere to be washed up.

Thought about walking back through the trees, but decided to leave that for tomorrow, if I'm still here. Got dressed and walked slowly back to my stuff, with lots of stops to soothe my legs. They hurt so much all the time, even when I'm not walking. Counted the steps on the way back. No idea why I feel the need to know the size of my island, but I do. Six hundred and seven steps, end to end.

Bananas for lunch. Then I remembered the Skittles. I couldn't remember the last time I saw them, but eventually tracked them down, buried in sand, next to the rock where I had put them. I only ate one. Oh, the amazing sweetness, the mouthwateringness of that small red piece of magic. I will make them last as long as possible.

Tidied all my stuff up, put some of it back into the now dry suitcase and the rest on the flatter rocks.

The books have pretty much dried out, although it's hard to separate some of the pages. I should be building a shelter or a raft or something. Started reading Rose Madder.

Day five

Oh my god, the book is terrifying. I've never read anything like it before. Got to page twenty two and was sure that he was going to suddenly pull up next to her and drag her back home and kill her. I didn't realise that I was holding my breath until I started to hiccup. That used to happen when I was younger and watched Doctor Who on TV; this is so much worse. And then the pages were stuck together and I had to jump to page twenty seven. So I know she's still alive, but I have no idea how it happened and what he's doing and where he is now.

I have to read lying on my stomach because sitting up involves bending my legs. I lay a beach towel carefully over my legs to avoid even more burning. It hurts, but not as badly as bending them to sit up.

I should have been doing something constructive. I kept reading.

It got dark and I have no light, so I went to sleep. When I woke, I knew I should be doing something practical, like building a raft, but I wanted to start reading again straight away. I don't know why I'm not taking my situation seriously enough. I did know I needed to look for more food, though; bananas are not enough and anyway, I have this idea that if you eat nothing but bananas, you die or something. I might be imagining that. Maybe that's carrots.

Head still throbbing, but didn't take another pill. I need to make them last.

Saw two planes. Well, vapour trails really; a trillion miles away. Cried.

Spent the morning following the rock face as closely as possible without tripping over scrub or walking into trees. There are three more little waterfalls like mine, although none lead to pools except the one at the far end. Stopped at the far end for a drink and then walked back randomly, through the trees. It's not like a walk in the woods at home. I don't think there's a tree here that's taller than about twelve feet, and they are all quite straggly and stunted. Guess the soil's not great here. There are no proper paths and many of the trees are very close together, so I had to push myself through the undergrowth at some points.

I found pomegranates! Three trees, all with dozens of beautiful, ripe fruits on them. Four more banana trees. Some other yellowish fruit, shaped a bit like a plum, but harder. Two of those. A lemon tree. Very straggly and not healthy-looking. A source of vitamin C though. But doesn't all fruit have vitamin C in it? And three olive trees, all bunched closely together.

Lots of other trees and shrubs, some with fruits just starting to form, so I can't tell what they are yet. Berries, too, but I have no idea what they are so won't eat them. Unless I get desperate.

I won't pick any fruit until I need to eat it. I brought back one pomegranate and a banana for my lunch. Bashed the pomegranate open on a rock. Bliss. I won't starve, although a totally fruit-based diet is not going to be good for my digestive system.

Saw another plane. Too high, too far away. Swore at it.

Day eight

Have decided not to write every day, because paper is so scarce. If anyone is reading this, you may want to skip the next bit anyway. Bodily functions are not attractive.

Spent a whole day using sticks, fingers and the mask from the snorkel to dig a sort of toilet. It's a big, rectangular hole, close to a tree with a low branch. When I crouch down, I hang onto the branch to stop myself falling backwards into it. After I've been, I throw sand in, to cover the smell and try not to attract flies. I needed to get this sorted because the fruit diet is having a drastic effect on my system. The plan is that, when this toilet is full, if I'm still here, I shall dig another. To be honest, crouching to use the toilet is horrendously painful for my legs, but I've tried doing it standing up and you really don't want details of how that went.

I suppose you're wondering about toilet paper. I will explain here and then won't mention any of this stuff again. Don't want to use leaves because they're scratchy and could be poisonous. Have selected the three tattiest pairs of boxer shorts and am using them and then washing them out in the sea afterwards. It's a disgusting job but I can't see an alternative. Funny, they never tell you this stuff in books and films.

All the time, while I was digging, I tried to remember anything I have ever seen about making fire. There's a thing where you get a stick and twirl it backwards and forwards between your hands, while the bottom of it is on a rock (or is it another piece of wood?) with some bits of kindling. I've seen it done on TV but wasn't paying attention. I saw a thing once, about making fire with a lemon, but I think you need nails, or bits of copper or something.
Spent some time yesterday trying the thing with the twirly wood and failing. Have blisters on both hands now.

Day eleven

There are thirty four pages in this scrapbook, if you count the insides of the front and back covers. I am squashing about five hundred words onto each page. That means I can write about seventeen thousand words. Do I have that many words in me? Will I be here long enough to fill the book? The colours on the pages are all blended and merged, so I'm using different coloured pencils to make sure there's contrast and keep my words legible. I so want to draw but I cant afford to waste the space. All this wittering about word counts is a waste anyway though. Stop.

Finished reading Rose Madder. This is very important. If my body is eventually discovered here, I would like it buried with pages twenty two to twenty seven, one hundred and twenty three to one hundred and twenty six and two hundred and eight to two hundred and thirty three of Rose Madder, so that I can read them in whatever afterlife I may turn up in. On the other hand, if I get home safely, the first thing I will buy is a copy of the book.

Daily routine is something like this:

Breakfast; bananas or pomegranate and maybe one of the yellow things. I'm being careful with them because I don't know what they are, but they seem ok. I tried tasting a raw olive and it was disgusting. I'd have to be far more desperate than this.

Clean my teeth, with the smallest amount of toothpaste possible. I need to make it last.

Swim in the sea, clean my bruises and cuts and soak my sunburn, which is improving all the time, then float, face-down, with the snorkel and watch the fish. They are beautiful and so close, I could reach out and touch them.

Think about the twins

Think about coffee

Dry off, cover exposed areas with sunscreen, dress in a t-shirt with the charger cable belt.

Think I should build a shelter

Comb my hair, which is getting more tangled every day

Wash yesterday's t-shirt

Tidy up (that doesn't take long)

Think about making a fire

Think about the twins

Think about other things to eat

Read book

Lunch (see breakfast)

Walk, either along the beach or among the trees.

Worry.

Think about Ellie and Dan

Think about fire

Think I should build a shelter

Wonder what will happen if summer ends and I am still here

Stand on the beach and look out to sea for ages, waiting for a ship

Worry

Wonder if I need a paracetamol.

Think I should build a raft.

Read book (reading Kiss the Girls now. V scary, but in a different way from Rose Madder). I would never have read any of this stuff before.

Supper (see breakfast, but with a Skittle for pudding)

Pack everything away into the suitcase
Bed

There is too much day, and not enough to do.

Day 14

Fell in the toilet.

Day 16

Who knew that the insides of banana peel are really soothing on sunburn and insect bites? Oh, have I not mentioned the insect bites? Too many to count. Driving me crazy and there are more every morning when I wake, especially on my feet and ankles.

Down to nine and a half paracetamol tablets. Head hurts all the time and I have been throwing up quite a bit.

All the pencils are getting shorter.

On a positive note, my legs are healing.

Day 19, I think. Should have been making five-barred gates. Too late now.

I am so stupid. There is nobody on this planet as stupid as me. I can not believe that I have spent all this time being stressed about fire and worrying about my fruit-based diet. Aaaaargh! Stupid, stupid, stupid.

Two days ago, I was playing house. I took some of the things, like the washing stuff, comb and reading glasses out of the suitcase and arranged them on a flattish rock, as though they were on a shelf in my bedroom. I made up my "bed"; one towel goes under and one over me and I have stuffed leaves into a pair of jeans to make a pillow. I wear the other pair to sleep in, with my cotton dress and the blue jacket and two pairs of socks. I'm sure I look lovely, but there's no mirror.

I tidied my kitchen (two cartons of water, a slowly diminishing packet of Skittles and some dried banana skins).

I decided to cut my tangled hair with the nail scissors. It was hard work and I hadn't got very far when I changed my mind and thought I would cut the mesh lining out of one of the pairs of swimshorts and see if there was a way to use it as a bag to collect fruit in. I've been thinking I could collect and mash up smaller berries and stuff, to make paint and maybe paint on the rocks. So, there I was, standing with this net bag in my hand, having tied together a couple of the loose ends at the bottom, and I just thought, "this is a fishing net". How had I not considered the fish as a source of food? I see them every day. Of course they're beautiful, but this is about survival. If I can find a way to catch them, I'll have a much more balanced diet. And now I have a fishing net, or at least, the beginnings of one.

Saw a plane. Ignored it.

It took a while to find a bendy stick that I could weave through the top part of my net, to make a firmer rim that would stay open under water, but I did it. By that time, I was really excited and stripped off and jumped into the water with my snorkel and net.

Of course, I didn't catch anything, but I know I will. I just need to keep trying and be patient. They came very close and a couple of the little silver ones went just inside the net, but I moved too quickly and scared them off.
Eventually, I gave up and came out of the water, and that's when the real magic happened. I reached over to pick up the comb, which had been lying beneath the reading glasses, and it was so hot that it was sticky where it had started to melt. Of course it was! The sun had been shining down, through the lens of the glasses, onto the comb. The language I used as I

screamed at myself was interesting – some, I think I may have made up. How did I not see this as soon as I found the glasses? How did I not immediately understand that I had fire, right there in my hands?

I am the wrong person. Whoever is in charge of the universe has completely misunderstood who I am. They should have cast some big strong Girl Guide leader, someone who knows how to survive by catching their own food, knitting their own yoghurt, building a shelter out of a pair of flip-flops and a hairband. Not me. My skills lie elsewhere. I paint. If I could do magic, I would crush berries and use them to paint a raft on the cliff face and then make it real and sail away on it. Or I could paint a flare-gun or a shelter, or, at the very least, a cave where I could hide from the sun. Or rain, presumably, at some point.

Day twentysomething

Fire is magic. It was so easy. I was very controlled; went and collected loads of small stuff for kindling, pine needles and twigs and dead leaves, and then went back for larger stuff, dead branches and sticks. A lot of the trees are so straggly that it's easy to pull bits off. I pulled away at them until I had a huge pile on the beach.

I used a couple of pages from the dried-out puzzle book, mixed in with tiny twigs and pine needles, to get it started. One minute I was holding the glasses, tilting the lens to get the right angle, the next there was a brown scorch-mark on the paper and then there was fire!

Everything feels different with fire. I have light, heat, comfort. I also still have a headache and I think some of my bites may be infected but I've taken two paracetamol to celebrate and I won't think about that today.

Caught two tiny silver fish. Couldn't bear to hit them with a stick to make them die. Not worried about cruelty -- can't make myself care about that. I just didn't want to spoil them, smash them up so there was nothing worth eating. I dropped them on a rock, still in the net, and looked the other way until they stopped flapping about.

Poked a stick through the first one and held it over the fire. When the stick burnt through, the fish fell in and I had to shovel it out with another piece of wood.

I burned my fingertips, grabbing it and scraping the skin off with the scissors, but I couldn't wait. I used my fingers to eat it, shoving the tiny pieces of charred flesh into my mouth, eating as much as I could while carefully avoiding the head and the insides. Maybe one day I will be that desperate, but not today. It was so small but so wonderful. With the second one, I just put it into the edge of the fire, where the flames had died down, and turned it over a few times with a stick. It took hardly any time to cook and was just as delicious as the first one. I threw the scraps back into the sea.

When the sun went down it somehow felt wrong sitting by the fire on my own. There should be more people and we should be telling stories or singing. Someone should have a guitar. Maybe there should be a couple of those candles holders that you stick into the sand, with insect-repelling candles fluttering in them. We should be toasting marshmallows over the fire, on long sticks, and drinking beer.

Got the blue bunny out of the suitcase and sat her next to me. Got a stick, stuck it in the ground on the other side of me and hung the baseball cap on it. Now I had two friends. Talked to them about the twins. They are in my head and heart every waking moment. I told them how, at twenty-three, I thought Graham was the love of my life, that we would be together forever. How, the day after I told him that I was pregnant, he suddenly got an urgent call from the mother he hadn't seen in years, and disappeared from my life in an instant. Never called, never texted, never responded to my calls, texts, letters. We had no Facebook in those days, no Twitter, none of the online presence we take for granted now. He just vanished from my life. He'd been signing on, so there wasn't even a place of work I could contact. I'd never met his family, had no idea how to contact them. I'd always assumed there was plenty of time for that. I cried a lot but it never once occurred to me that I might not keep my baby.

I told my new friends how, in the fifth month, when I knew there were two babies and was already so enormous that I expected to explode at any moment, my boss, Aimee, told me that I wasn't really what people visiting a trendy gallery off the Kings Road expected to see. I no longer "fitted". My job as her assistant, supposed to be my way into the world of art, to prepare me for when I was a great artist myself, was gone. She felt sorry for me though, so she gave me some publicity stuff to do from home, and she called round a few friends. By the time the twins were born, I had a steady stream of work, writing press releases, brochures and blurb for exhibitions, and I had also started to do some proof-reading for a small publishing firm owned by Aimee's cousin. It was erratic but I got by, and I could work from my tiny, rented flat, so I didn't have to leave the babies with anyone else. Caitlin helped out when she was home from uni. I shelved my dream of becoming an artist, believing that I would come back to it once the children were older.

I wittered on to my friends about feeding, teething, first steps, broken sleep, chicken pox, tantrums, and then I thought, if I'm going to talk to the bunny and hatman about all this stuff, they should have names. I am calling the bunny Min and hatman Joe.

I told Min and Joe about the amazing fortieth birthday gift that Caitlin, Sam, Ellie and Dan had bought for me. A two week artist's retreat in Crete with a focus on water-colours. There would be classes before lunch and then free time so that we could wander and paint to our heart's content. I have never, ever regretted the changes I made in order to take care of the twins, but I still had my dream, and they all knew that. They also knew about my fear of flying, but they believed, and they were right, that this would be the incentive I needed to try and deal with it. And I did. I paid for therapy, workshops, books. I researched online, I did everything I could, so that, when the day came, I was able to walk onto the plane as if it was the most natural thing in the world. Inside, things were not quite so calm, but no-one would have known.

It turns out, I was right all along.

We chatted for quite a while before I went to bed. Well, ok, *I* chatted. Min and Joe didn't say anything. They're not real. I'm lonely, not crazy.

Another day

Just what I needed. My period started today. That should make it possible for me to work out exactly how long I've been here, but there's something going on in my brain and I can't clear the fog enough to calculate the days. Not important. Have made arrangements by cutting up a the last two unused pairs of boxer shorts. Won't mention this when it happens again. Waste of pencil and paper.

Saw a ship and a plane. Fucking miles away. Didn't wave.

Have eaten fish and fruit most days. The fish are almost all the tiny, silver ones. Sardines, perhaps. How should I know. Sardines come in tins, not flapping about on a rock. I caught a bigger fish yesterday but I panicked when it took so long flapping about on the rock and I threw it back into the sea.

Spend a lot of time thinking about the twins. Starting to believe I might never see them again. Cry a lot. Min cuddles me. Joe's not really cuddly and anyway, sometimes I wear the hat and then he disappears.

Always hungry, but not starving.

Worried about the fire. We must be well into September now and it's still warm, but some days there's a lot less sun. If the fire goes out, the sun is the only thing I can use to light it again. In the daytime, I keep it fairly low, but I build it up high at night, to make sure it stays alight. Have discovered that, even if it goes out, the ashes stay hot for quite a while, so in the morning, if I put some paper (sorry, Jacqueline Wilson) and a few bits of kindling onto the ashes and then fan them with a book, I can get it re-lit. But what if it rains?

Next day

Today, for the first time, it occurred to me that the cabin crew should have checked the toilets before they evacuated the plane. Can't blame them for getting out as quickly as possible. But can't help thinking things could be so different if they had found me.

Daily routine now something like this:

Breakfast. Fish, if I can be bothered. If not, fruit, which is all getting a bit past it.
Think about home, Ellie, Dan, Caitlin.
Cry
Wash and clean my teeth, if I feel like it. There's no shower gel or shampoo left and only a tiny bit of toothpaste.
Worry about what will happen when the weather changes
Talk to Min. Not bothering with Joe anymore because I like to wear the hat
Worry about what will happen when all the fruit is gone.
Re-read one of the books. Maybe when (if) I get home, I can go on Mastermind. Specialist subject, Rose Madder by Stephen King.
Worry that I will die here and no-one will ever know
Look at the safety razors, travel iron, flip-flops and sandals and try to be inspired. Fail to think of anything they could be useful for
Sit and stare at a lemon. I know there's a way to make fire with them
Wash some clothes, if I can be bothered
Try different ways to make the olives edible. Currently soaking some in a juice carton
Collect wood for the fire
Cry

Could be Friday

It was really windy last night. I covered my face with a t-shirt but still didn't sleep well. This morning there's sand in everything, Min had been blown right across the beach and was wedged against a rock and the fire was out. Rescued Min. Took me ages to start the fire again, because there were clouds first thing and I had to wait for the sun to come out.

Also, the wind had churned up the sea so that, when I went to catch fish, everything was really murky and I couldn't see under the surface. It will clear, and meanwhile there's still fruit, but it's another thing to worry about. Fruit is seasonal. Sooner or later I will have eaten everything or it will have rotted, and then there will be nothing except fish, so I don't need obstacles in the way of my fish-catching.

Really need to think about building a shelter or getting away.

Plan A: cut down six trees, using the nail scissors, tie them together using the phone charger lead, attach the travel iron as a rudder, use a pair of jeans as a sail and set off for home.

Plan B: cut down loads of branches and stuff using the nail scissors, bind them together with the phone charger cable and prop them against the rock-face. Make mud from sand and water and fill in the gaps. Hey presto! Wind and rainproof shelter.

Plan C: just start swimming and try and go in a straight line, using the sun as a guide.

Plan D: stay here and die

Cheered myself up by shaving my legs and armpits. Smooth legs won't help me get away from here, but they make me feel better.

Tuesday (why not?)

A turtle swam past this morning and I reached automatically for my phone in my back pocket, to take a photo.

Friday

Feels like a Friday. I have been ill. All the paracetamols are gone. A couple of the insect bites on my left foot were infected. I wash them in salt water all the time and try to keep the sand out and I do try not to scratch them, but sometimes I can't help it, I do it in my sleep. My ankle was swollen and painful and I had a temperature and a headache. I dragged the beach towel close to the sea, took three paracetamols and then lay on the towel, with my feet in the water, and dozed in and out of sleep.

I dreamed.

Ellie was screaming at me to get out of her room and stop interfering with her life, but I couldn't find the door and I couldn't explain to her because I couldn't remember the words I needed. She melted into a puddle on the carpet and then trickled out under the door that I couldn't see.

I was listening to the Eurythmics and trying to sing along to Sweet Dreams, but I had a huge lump of bubble-gum in my mouth and my teeth were stuck together. The more of it I pulled out, the more there was.

Min was biting my ankles. I kicked her away and as she flew into the distance, she sprouted glowing, golden wings and just kept going, skimming above the water. I wanted to follow her, but I was buried up to my knees in the sand.

I found a payphone attached to the cliff face and tried really hard to make a reverse charge call to Caitlin but I couldn't remember her number and the operator only spoke Welsh.

Woke in the night, freezing cold, although my head was still burning up. Dragged the towel away from the water and curled up next to the fire. Woke to the smell of burning. Thank god the towel was wet. One corner of it is all singed, but it could have been so much worse. Rolled away from the fire and went back to sleep.

Dan was standing on the water, several feet away from the beach, calling to me, but I was afraid. When I did stand up and walk towards him, the sea was frozen and I slipped and fell through the ice. The ice sealed above my head and I clawed frantically at it, but it wouldn't break.

Woke up freezing cold again. Rolled back towards the fire, which was dying down but still hot.

Woke up burning up all over. Sun was beating down on me. Rolled down to the water, soaked the towel, then crawled back up the beach, wrapped the towel around myself and fell asleep again.

Not sure how long that went on, waking, sleeping, freezing, burning, dreaming, but this morning I woke up feeling loads better. My feet look as though I've been sitting in the bath for a week, all wrinkled and flubby, but the bites are clean and the swelling has gone down. Also, my headache has completely gone and I feel that I'm thinking clearly for the first time since I got here. All the paracetamols are gone. I don't remember taking them, but the empty packet is here, so I suppose I must have.

The fire was out when I woke, but the sun was up and I got it going again in a few minutes. I'm getting good at this. I need the fire to be there. Without it, life is even more bleak. Caught some fish and ate them so fast that I gave myself hiccups and indigestion.

I was very weak and wobbly for a few days, didn't really go anywhere or do anything, except catch a few fish and pick bananas and pomegranates. Had a go at reading some of the Jacqueline Wilson, but I'm just not young enough to engage with it. Re-read Rose Madder. What's weird is that, even knowing exactly what happens all the way through, it still terrifies me.

Haven't walked farther than the pomegranate trees or swum for longer than it takes to catch a couple of fish for days, but I have more energy today. Swam out as far as I feel safe. The water close to the shore is very calm and seems to have no tidal changes, but about twenty strokes out, I start feeling an undertow and it's much harder to swim, so I always turn back at that point. Walked among the trees for a bit; feeling much better now, so I will walk to the other end of the beach again tomorrow.

Another day

Fuck, fuck, fuck, fuck, fuck. There would be a lot more fucks if I wasn't worried about running out of pages.

People. Have. Been. Here. Fucking real, live, human people, here on my island and I missed them!

It's not my fault that I haven't been walking much since my foot started to get infected, I know that. But why didn't I pull myself together sooner and get a grip, walk along the beach yesterday, or the day before? Why did I wait so long? To be honest, I nearly decided not to even go today, but I have this sort of hope that maybe another suitcase has been washed up. With clothes that fit, and a matches and a torch. And, who knows, perhaps the boatful of provisions and chickens and goats has arrived. What is this obsession with goats, anyway?

The first thing I noticed, as I walked along the beach, was that the wind the other night had obliterated all my previous footprints. It was like walking on fresh snow, and I wandered in circles and spirals, making footprint patterns as I went. Tried to write my name, but it was too long and I got bored after three letters.

I was so focused on watching my feet and the patterns I was making, that it was only when I almost stepped into a long, shallow trench in the sand that I stopped abruptly and looked up. I had reached the other end of the beach without even noticing and there were several deep grooves in the sand, leading up out of the water. It took a moment for me to understand that this was where canoes or kayaks had been pulled up to prevent them floating away. The sand close to the water was churned up with footprints and boatprints but I thought I could make out eight separate boats. So, at least eight people. More if they were twin-seated. Further up the beach, closer to the trees, there were footprints and other disturbed places where people had obviously sat down, perhaps to rest or eat. There was a half-hearted attempt at a sand-castle. There were the ashes of a fire.

I don't know how long I stood there, just staring, trying to wrap my brain around the fact that real, live people had actually been here. Why didn't I hear them? Ok, it's six hundred and seven steps from my base to this end of the beach, but it's quiet here, surely sound would travel? And then I understood that they must have been here while I was sick, asleep; even if I had heard them I'd probably have thought I was dreaming.

Why didn't they go for a walk along the beach? Why didn't they go in amongst the trees and see footprints, broken branches, my amazing toilet arrangements? Perhaps they did and just assumed it was from other groups like theirs.

A group of people have been on a canoeing or kayaking trip and stopped off here for a break and then gone away again.

I have never felt such despair.

I dropped to my knees on the sand and then lay down full-length in one of the furrows created by a boat, staring up at the sky. I wanted to cry, to scream. I wanted to rush into the water and swim after them, yelling at them to come back, save me, take me home. I wanted them to have accidentally left a kayak behind, or a mobile phone, or a cigarette lighter. Or a sandwich.

I lay there for a long time, until the dampness from the sand started to seep into my bones and the sun was starting to go down. Got up and hobbled around for a while to get the blood flowing again, and then tried to get something of a grip while there was still some daylight.

They might very well have left something behind, these invisible people. I crawled carefully up and down the beach, trying to imitate the fingertip searches you see on detective shows, sifting the sand through my fingers, looking for anything they might have dropped or forgotten. I was crying with anger and frustration, the whole time. Nothing stays right. One thing works out so then immediately a balance has to be struck by something going wrong. But this was so cruel, I had been so close to rescue. I still had not thought about the reality of trying to save myself. How many times had I thought I should sort out a shelter or something, and then done nothing? Millions. Because, deep down, until this moment, I had really believed that someone would come, someone would take me home.

I found three cigarette ends, carefully buried in one small hole. In spite of looking very carefully all around them, I couldn't find the box of matches or cigarette lighter that I really wanted. I found an empty plastic wrapper that may have held a sandwich, but the writing's in Greek, so who knows? I found a plastic fork. I found a bone; I think it's the remains of a chicken drumstick. Just inside the trees, I spotted a few pieces of tissue. I didn't investigate further. Shame they didn't leave the rest of the roll or the packet or whatever.

They were very tidy. They stopped here for their picnic, then they cleared up after themselves and left.

I have never felt so alone as I did at that moment, standing on the beach in the footprints of strangers, staring around me at the evidence of their visit.

I came back to my base, built up the fire and tried to think. They might come back and, if they did, I should be ready for them. If this is a regular stopping-off place for boat people, then there are two things that tells me; I am probably within half a day's paddling distance of civilisation and people know that this island exists

Perhaps I should relocate to the other end of the island. But what if, next time, they stop at this end? If I relocate, I need to leave some kind of message here to tell people to look for me. Not sure how to do that. A note could blow away or get rained on, and writing in the sand isn't going to work. Have to think of something, though.

Is it even worth bothering? What's the point? It was probably the last trip of this year anyway. It's really cloudy today. Will build the fire up and go to sleep.

Next evening (I really must get a grip of what day it is, but how?)

Am fighting the desire to just give up and not do anything; making a decision is so hard. Spent the day on the main part of the beach, pacing from one end to the other, terrified that the boat people might return and not see me. I didn't even want to take the time to go looking for fruit, in case I missed something. Couldn't make my mind up what to do. Tired, sad, desperately lonely. Even talking to Min didn't cheer me up. Joe's gone for good, because I'm wearing the hat most of the time. Stared and stared at the sea. Perhaps there's land there and I'm just not seeing it. If I could see land, however far away, I would swim towards it, but I can't. I need to get out past the rocks at one of the ends of the beach and try and see behind the cliff face. But it's so hard to swim when I get that far out, and I'm afraid I might not be able to get back.

Tomorrow

Last night was beautifully clear, and the clouds all disappeared. I lay on the sand and stared up at the stars, wishing I knew something about the constellations. I am so the wrong person to be here. The right person would look at the stars and calculate exactly where they were and then swim off in the right direction and be home in time for tea.

By the time I curled up and fell asleep, I had decided I would move to the other end of the beach, but there was quite a lot I needed to do first. Started as soon as I woke up this morning, before lethargy overtook me. I needed to bring the fire with me, so took a while trying to work out how to do that. I eventually decided I should have a fire at each end. That means I'll need to walk backwards and forwards at least once a day, probably twice, to keep both fires going, but it might be worth it. If anyone comes here, they will know I'm here if they see a fire, even if I'm not close to it. Also, if one goes out, the other may still be ok. Once I'm sorted, perhaps I'll have a fire half-way along the beach as well.

This is how I took the fire to my new base.

I took a long branch that was burning at one end and started walking along the beach with it. That didn't work, because the flames blew back towards me and anyway, It looked as though it would burn down before I was even half way there. I had another think.

About thirty paces from my base, I built a small fire on the beach with wood and kindling. Then I went back to the fire at my base and pulled out a long stick that was burning well, carried it carefully to the newly-laid fire and used it to set that alight. I repeated this, again and again, not worrying when the earlier fires started to go out, as long as I had one to take fire from and transfer it to the next. I stopped frequently, staring out to sea in case I was missing something. This would all be unnecessary if the kayaks came back now.

It was early afternoon by the time I had a fire going where I wanted it, close to the rock pool at the far end of the beach. I built it up hugely, not wanting it to go out while I was away, and then walked back to get my stuff, watching the horizon all the time. Just in case.

It was hard to leave. It's not as though I've been happy here, but this has been my safe place. It's where I live. But it's not where the boat people stopped. I packed everything into the suitcase, except the books and pencils and the reading glasses, which went into the rucksack on my back. I built the fire up as much as possible before I left. I said goodbye to my waterfall. I wished there was something I could do that would leave a permanent message, just in case the fire went out and visitors just assumed it had been built by people like them. I wanted a pen-knife, to carve words into a tree. I had a bit of a go with the nail scissors but it was pointless.

It took forever to drag the suitcase along the beach to my new place. My shoulders and arms ached and I stopped more and more frequently. As I dragged it, the suitcase dug a trench and eventually it would get so deep that I couldn't go any further, so I would have to wrench it out and start again. So much for the pristine beach of a few days ago. Looking back along the beach, it looked as though some huge, legless animal had been dragging itself along. The stuff of nightmares. Every time I stopped, I gazed out to sea, wishing with my whole being that I would see a boat, heading towards me, coming to save me. I still wasn't thinking about saving myself.

Made my bed, close to the cliff face. It's not so protected here, because I don't have the rock rooms.

Dug a new toilet. Each time I do this, it takes longer. Is this because I am less motivated or am I getting weaker? I've definitely lost weight, and haven't really felt totally ok since I was ill. I'm so thin that my knickers keep sliding down, so I hardly ever bother to wear them now. The t-shirts were huge anyway, but now I really struggle to keep them on my shoulders. The only thing that's vaguely comfortable is my cotton dress, because, although it's too big now, it just sort of hangs on me, but it doesn't fall off.

It's getting colder and there's a feeling in the air of rain. Put almost all the clothes on to go to sleep. Writing this by firelight. There's half a page left in the scrapbook and then I shall write round the edges of the pages in Sleepovers, the other Jacqueline Wilson book.

I have a plan. Tomorrow, I will swim out past the rocks, as far as I can, and then try and go round to the back of the island, along the side of the cliff. The waves are stronger and I am worried about getting back, but I'm thinking there could be land in that direction and it might be really close. The boat people must have come from somewhere. I have to try. Just need to pack everything away in the suitcase, then bed. Goodnight Min.

Have pretty much given up trying to remember days.

My plan to swim to the back of the island was literally washed out. I woke up in the middle of the night soaking wet, rain pouring down. The fire was almost out and there was no moon, so I stumbled about in the dark as I dragged the suitcase and my bedding across to the trees. It was still wet in there, the trees don't offer a lot of protection, but it was better than being out in the open. Thank god I always put everything into the suitcase before I go to sleep.
I sat on the suitcase, under a small tree, wrapped in the wet towels, hugging my knees, head down, and waited for the rain to stop.

It didn't.

I thought I was wet through already, but as water poured through the trees and dripped from the branches, soaking through the towels and all my clothes, dripping down my neck, between my breasts, trickling between my thighs and pooling round my feet, I began to really understand what that meant. There was no part of me that wasn't wet and growing colder by the second. Any movement seemed to relocate a pool of water that might have collected in a fold of the towels or a crease in my clothes and redistribute it to another part of my body. I tried to keep still, which became less difficult as my muscles began to cramp and stiffen.

With my body immobile, my mind flew all over the place.

I was clutching the towels around me, even though they were soaking wet. I wondered why I bothered, and flashed back to a summer on the beach in Cromer, when the twins were six. Around sixish, when most people had headed home for their tea, we would still be on the beach and I would go into the sea to swim. For some reason, because the water was cooler at that time of day, I went into the water in my cotton trousers and t-shirt, because I didn't want to be cold. It made no scientific sense and the children laughed at me, but I did it every day. And now, the same feeling of comfort was being provided by soaking wet, freezing cold towels.

I thought about the first night Dan and Ellie spent apart, when they were seven and Ellie went for a sleepover with a friend. Dan was up and down all night, unable to sleep, and eventually crawled in with me. Ellie apparently slept soundly through the night.

The time, when they were eight, when Ellie hit the stop button at the bottom of an escalator in John Lewis, just as we were getting off it. Dan was horrified but jealous too. He would have liked to have had the courage to do something so daring and wicked.

Dan's first clarinet solo, when he was nine. He only played a few bars, and then the rest of the class joined in again, but no-one could hear them properly because Ellie was standing on her seat, clapping and cheering. She didn't stop until I dragged her down and squashed her back into her seat.

Caitlin's face, when she first saw my babies. And when I asked her to be their not-godmother. And the way she was so thrilled when they first stayed overnight with her and survived.

Sam, Caitlin, Ellie and Dan waving as I went through security towards the departure lounge.

Blood on the mirror.

The rhythm of the raindrops hitting the branches around me began to remind me of something. I focused for a while and then found myself reciting from something we had to learn in German class when I was about thirteen; Wer reitet so spät durch Nacht und Wind? No idea what it comes from or who wrote it, and I could only remember four lines and the rhythm. Can't even remember what it means. Also, had to recite it in my head because my teeth were chattering so much that I couldn't speak.

Trying to remember the words was good for me, taking my mind away from what was happening to my body. Once I'd given up trying to get a grip on the rest of the German thing, I moved on to the lyrics of songs I've known. Only in my head, but that's probably better than the way it would sound if I sang them out loud. I Will Always Love You sounded amazing inside my head and I remembered nearly all the words. The Dolly version, not Whitney Houston. I flashed back to a documentary about why Dolly wrote it and remembered crying when I watched it. Too cold to cry now.

I worked my way through several Abba numbers and quite a lot of Madonna. When I couldn't remember the words, I made them up. Eventually, my brain went the same way as my body, and shut down. No more songs.

It was still raining when dawn came, just beating down steadily as though it would never end. I hadn't moved. For a while I had been cold, but, at some point in the night, I moved past that point. There was no feeling and no longer much coherent thought. I waited.

As dawn broke, I tried to bring myself back to life. I raised my head with difficulty, working to unlock the necessary muscles, and peered out through the rain and the undergrowth to where my bed had been. The pool at the base of the cliff face had expanded and now took up most of the area where I had been sleeping. The fire might never have been there at all. There was a small blue shape bobbing about in the water and I realised I had left Min behind. It was only when I tried to stand up and retrieve her that I realised how bad things were. I couldn't unwrap my arms from around my knees. I couldn't move any part of my body, I was locked in place.

I focused on one finger on my right hand, tightening and releasing the muscles in it, again and again, until I was able to lift it and wriggle it. I did it again and again, with each finger, then with my wrists and arms, then toes, ankles, knees, until finally, I struggled to my feet. The whole process had been painfully slow. Pain screamed through my shoulders and down my back. It took months to remind myself how to take first one step and then another. Walking didn't feel like something I had been doing for forty years, it was something I had to teach myself, one tiny step at a time.

I was so wet already that I assumed wading into the pool to pick up Min couldn't possibly make it worse. I was wrong, of course. Just as I took the first, tentative step into the water, I was gripped by a tremendous cramp in my right calf. I screamed and fell forward, full-length into the pool.

Back under the trees again, soaked and freezing, I clutched a soggy blue rabbit and cried. I think I may have slept for a while.

The rain stopped, but the sun didn't come out. Without it, I had no way of working out whether it was morning or afternoon. I might have been there for one hour or eight. Whatever, it was time to try and warm up. This time, I moved more cautiously, stretching my muscles gently before dragging the suitcase out into the open. Even though there was no sun, the air was warm, but I felt that the cold in my limbs would never leave. I wanted fire. Every part of me ached and the signals between my brain and my fingers were slow and erratic.

I was wearing most of the clothes and it took forever to take them all off. My fingers had forgotten what buttons were. As I removed them, I spread the clothes across the wet sand, hoping that the sun would put in an appearance before night fell. Then, naked and still freezing cold, I opened the suitcase. The only clothes inside it were my bra, one t-shirt, the smart shirt, which I somehow so far had felt unable to spoil by taking it out of it's wrapping, and a giant pair of shorts. I struggled with the tiny plastic bits that hold the shirt in position in its wrapping, and stabbed myself twice on pins, but although I could see tiny spots of blood, I didn't feel a thing.

I dressed in the shorts, t-shirt, shirt and baseball cap. I am so skinny now, that even though I threaded the phone charger lead through the belt loops on the shorts and tied it tight, they still kept falling down, but at least I was a little warmer. The shirt is huge and I have rolled the sleeves up, but they keep coming unrolled. Once I was certain that my legs wouldn't give up on me, I ran up and down the beach, waving my arms and flapping the shirtsleeves, trying to get warm and bring myself back to life. I had to flap one arm at a time because I needed to hold on to the shorts to stop them falling down and tripping me up. I started singing again, trying to remember all the lyrics to Bat Out of Hell.

Picture this. Crazy woman, wearing huge shorts and shirt, tangled hair different lengths all the way round (I'm still trying to cut it but I get bored easily and the scissors are getting blunter) sticking out from under a Red Sox hat, running, arms windmilling, screaming "like a sinner before the gates of Heaven, I'll come crawling on back to yooooooo" at the top of her voice. If a boat turned up now, they'd put it into reverse and speed off into the distance without looking back.

It did warm me up though. Very tired now.

Two days later

The nights have been the hardest. None of the clothes have dried out properly, because the sun has stayed firmly behind the clouds and there's very little breeze. I still have no fire and I sleep curled up under some bushes at the edge of the beach. Things crawl on me but I find I don't squeal and run about as I once would have. It's not that I don't hate them, want to leap up and run screaming, I just don't have the energy. I am so tired.

I haven't been able to fish because the sea is all churned up and I can't see anything.

In the daytime, I stretch my muscles and run about, even though it's the last thing I want to do. And I sing. I don't know why I didn't do that before, but now I work on remembering the lyrics to songs I used to know. The earworms creep in though. I find myself singing Ice, Ice Baby, even though they are the only words I know from that song and it drives me crazy. And Do They Know it's Christmas is lurking beneath every song I have ever loved and leaps out at me when I least expect it.

I'm hungry all the time. Most of the fruit I was eating before the rain came has fallen from the trees and is starting to rot. I'm picking up and eating what I can but I can't bear the thought of being ill again, on top of everything else. I've tried a few small berries that I was avoiding before, and they may be ok. They're bitter but so far haven't made me sick. I've even eaten a couple of olives, but they are so disgusting. I wish the water would clear so that I can fish again.

At last, today, the sun has come back, weak but definitely there. I am sitting on the sand, writing. The scrapbook is full, so I've started on Jacqueline Wilson. I'm writing round and round the edges of the pages. The best ones are the beginnings and endings of chapters, where there's more blank space. All the pencils are very small now.

Had a go at writing with a bit of burnt wood from the fireplace, just to see if that would work. After all, isn't that how charcoal is made? I used one of the pages from the puzzle book. Just made a lot of grubby splotches on the paper. No discernible words.

I have a load of kindling and small sticks spread across the sand to dry so that I can start a fire if the sun stays out long enough. A couple of t-shirts are nearly dry, but the towels are taking ages. The expanded pool of water has seeped away but I won't make the mistake of sleeping over there again.

Sunday

I'm calling it Sunday because the sun is the most wonderful thing in the universe.

I have fire again, but just at this end. I'm so tired; can't be bothered to walk all the way down the other end and build another one. The fire's pretty smoky because the wood is all wet, but I've dragged out some more onto the beach to dry out. And perhaps someone will see the smoke. Or I could make smoke signals. The only Morse code I know if SOS, but I guess that's all I need. Who am I kidding? Even if I saw a ship or a plane, I'd be more likely to set fire to the towel than to create effective smoke signals. And from such a distance, that tiny piece of flame wouldn't attract anyone.

Most of the clothes are dry now and I've rigged up a couple of sort of triangle thingies with sticks and draped the towels over them, close enough to the fire to dry out but hopefully not close enough to catch fire.

Had a serious talk with myself. I will not survive here unless I have shelter and more food, and I need to find some way of making fire that doesn't depend on the sun. Instead of sitting around worrying and making lists and telling myself that I should do stuff, I need to actually do it. And now. I shouldn't wait until I'm desperate, or too weak to do anything. Ok, I am the wrong person, they made a mistake casting me in this role, but perhaps I have hidden depths. Hidden shallows, Ellie would say.

Spent ages farting around with bits of wood, trying to make fire. I need to do this now, while I already have fire and can take my time. After a huge amount of time and effort, I have splinters in both hands and blisters on both palms, two broken nails and no fire. I'm getting closer though. Still wondering about the thing with lemons, but I think the stick-twirling's going to be a success.

I started off by putting a little pile of kindling on a flat rock, then finding a thin stick and holding it upright, with the tip in the kindling and twirling it between my palms. That was a waste of time. The stick just kept slipping on the rock and flicking the kindling away, and I started developing the first of many blisters. Also, I couldn't see how a spark was supposed to happen, so I knew something was wrong.

Then I tried laying a piece of wood on the ground and using that instead of the rock. Same result. I knew this was nearly right, I'm sure I've seen it on TV. There's just some stupid detail that I didn't pay attention to. There was something I needed to remember. Something that would stop the stick slipping away.

I left it for a few minutes and went to put wood on the fire. As I chucked a bundle of sticks on, one of them attached itself to my flapping shirt-sleeve because there was a deep crack in it that had trapped the cloth. I shook my arm hard, to release the stick, so that it fell into the fire and I snatched my arm away, as the flames started to lick at my sleeve. Then I realised what I'd thrown away and I reached straight into the fire without thinking, to grab the stick again. I had to hop around beating out flames on my sleeve, but they were only small and I didn't burn myself. I ran to the water and dipped my arm in to put it out properly. I wasn't hurt but I don't think I'd have felt anything even if I had been burned. Too excited.

I took my prize over to where I'd been trying to make fire. I stuffed some of the kindling into the crack in the wood, then laid it on the ground, knelt on the ends of it to keep it still, I I still have tiny holes on my knees, made by the bark) pushed the end of my thin stick into the crack until it was gripped and started twirling it between my palms again, ignoring the blisters and splinters in my excitement.

The stick didn't slip. Nothing much happened at first and I tried twirling even faster, although my hands were screaming at me to stop. And then, just as I was about to give up, I saw a tiny wisp of smoke, rising from the kindling and, there and gone so quickly that I might have imagined it, one lone spark.

I had to stop, because I couldn't hold the stick any longer, but now I believe I will be able to make fire. I see how it can be done; I just have to find a way of keeping a supply of wood and kindling dry, even in the rain. I've washed my hands in the sea and wrapped them in wet pieces of boxer shorts, but they're still stinging. It's not easy to hold the pencil. Will pack up and go to bed now. Am trying to remember all the words to We are the Champions.

There's been no more rain for a few days, but it's not as hot as it was and sometimes there's no sun. Reading back through my journal, I see the lists I made, saying how worried I was about food, shelter, fire, getting away from here. But I didn't *do* anything about any of it. That was incredibly stupid because I was stronger and healthier then and could probably have done more if I'd made the effort. I just couldn't allow myself to believe that I would still be here after all this time. I was holding onto the idea of rescue, so the need to take action for myself wasn't real. Surely a plane or helicopter or fishing boat would turn up and whisk me away?

No-one has come to save me though and I think that I finally believe that it's going to be up to me. Yes, the boat people might come back, but it must be well into autumn now, so they probably won't come until at least the spring. Maybe not until summer. I have to do things for myself. And I have to do them now, while I still can.

I took stock yesterday morning.

I have lost so much weight that even my own original clothes hang off me so much that they remind me of school uniforms at the beginning of a new school year. My mother seemed to expect me to grow into them overnight but it took months of trailing round with blazer cuffs hanging over my hands and my skirts rolled over at the waistband, before I felt comfortable.

I am brown all over; the sort of beautiful, even tan that many women would pay huge amounts of money for. Look closer though. See the tight, pale scar tissue behind my knees and down the backs of my thighs. I can't see at the top of my legs properly, but I can feel. I don't remember when the pain stopped but I will always have this reminder.

All my cuts and scrapes from the first few days have healed well, including the long one on my arm. Only the scars tell some of the story of what I have been through. The bump on my head disappeared weeks ago but I can't see what the scar looks like. My ankles and feet are covered in tiny pale scars from insect bites but I don't get many new ones now. That might be the change in the weather, or perhaps my blood doesn't taste so good any more. My hands are blistered and splintered but they'll heal. My nails are a mess. I keep breaking them and they seem to have become very brittle. I trim them and tidy them up with the nail scissors after they break, but it's happening more and more. My broken nails snag on clothes and leaves and stuff, and scratch me.

I have horrendous ~~diarh~~, ~~diorrho~~. Bugger, can't spell it. But you probably get the idea. I've eaten nothing but pretty manky fruit for the last few days, but the sea is clearing and I'm hoping for fish tomorrow.

My hair is a tangled, dried-out disaster. The plastic comb broke ages ago, and fingers are just not good enough. The nail scissors aren't very sharp and only cut a few hairs at a time anyway, so now I've started working my way round my head with one of the safety razors. It sort of works if I pull a chunk of hair out tightly with one hand and then slide the razor along it. I'm probably creating a billion split ends but, let's face it, that doesn't even make the top fifty in my list of problems right now.

I am very, very tired all the time. Everything seems to require so much effort and I just don't have the energy. I'm not sleeping well. Every sound wakes me, and I am constantly afraid that the rain will come again. I'm sleeping closer to the trees, but not amongst them. I've got a cough.

I haven't seen a gecko for days, no idea where they've gone. I've tried hard not to frighten them because I'm pretty sure they eat insects, and we've co-existed quite happily, but I don't think they like the change in the weather.

I have finally managed to make fire without the sun. This is my proudest achievement since waking up on the beach. It takes quite a long time and I can't imagine a time when I will be able to do it without causing splinters and blisters, but I can do it. I have done it three times in the last few days, just to check that it's real.

I laid out all my belongings. I still have

all the clothes, and the rags I've made from the boxer shorts
the three novels
a bundle of pages from the puzzle book and My Sister Jodie
four coloured pencil stubs (the blue one is finished)
one normal pencil stub
a pencil sharpener
a green hairband
the snorkel
the Nintendo game thingy
an eraser
Min
Two giant beach towels, one with a burnt corner
A rucksack
Sandals and flip-flops
A toothbrush
Empty containers from the shampoo, sun lotion and shower gel
An empty toothpaste tube
Adaptors
The phone charger lead
The travel iron
The disposable razors
My precious reading glasses
The nail scissors
The scrapbook, which is completely used up
This book, which is rapidly heading the same way
Oh, and the suitcase of course
And my fishing net

Also, for some reason, I still have the squashed chocolate mini-roll. At first, I didn't eat it because it looks so disgusting and had obviously absorbed sea water where the wrapper was torn. Now, I tell myself that when I decide to eat this, I will know I am truly desperate. As long as I don't need it, I'm ok.

At night, I chuck everything except what I'm wearing into the suitcase to keep it dry and safe, but I have realised that, if I put it away more carefully, and leave out things that can't be damaged by the rain, like the empty shampoo and shower gel bottles, there is plenty of room to get other stuff in there as well. I now have two thick sticks with splits in them, a couple of longer, thin ones and a small bundle of dry kindling, wrapped in banana leaves and then zipped into the rucksack, tucked away in there. It's not much, but when it rains again, I will have fire as soon as it stops.

There are still olives on the trees and I used to work on ways to make them edible, but I gave up a while back. I had tried soaking them in water for ages, both fresh and salt, but it didn't make much difference. I tried splitting them open and leaving them in the sun, rubbing them in bits of fish, in case somehow the oil from the fish might make a difference; nothing helped. I need to think about this again, because soon they might be all I have. I sort of think that if I could cook them, it might help, so I have put some into the ashes at the edge of the fire and am keeping an eye on them. I soaked them first, in case that might help. What do I know? Olives come in glass bottles, or little plastic containers, stuffed with pimentos. You take them on picnics.

I closed my eyes and allowed myself a break from being organised. Behind my eyelids, I wandered up and down the supermarket aisles, picking up cheese, ham, yoghurt, wine, strawberries, grapes and warm bread for my picnic on the beach. I knew exactly where everything was. I picked up enough for all of us. I texted Dan and reminded him to bring the Frisbee. The canned music in the shop was playing Driving in my Car and I sang along.

It was a beautiful fantasy and I held it in my head for a while as I sat and gazed out over the water.

The truth is, I do have a plan, but it frightens me. I am going to try and swim round to the back of my island, but I'm trying not to think about it. The water is rougher than it was before the rain and sort of greyer, and I am exhausted just thinking about it. And as far as I can see, the rock face is almost sheer at this end so, once I start, I have to keep going or turn back, there's no stopping for a break. But I don't want to go all the way back to the other end of my world to check whether it's more promising there, because my fire and all my clothes are here and I will need them as soon as I get back. *If* I get back. I don't have the energy to drag stuff six hundred and seven steps to the other end, so I shall leave from here.

Before I go though, I want to make sure I have something to come back to. Because if I do come back, if I don't find anything out there, I will be here for a long time. And I will be exhausted.

Tomorrow, I shall make myself a place to go to when the rain comes again, because when I come back I may not have the energy. I have some ideas about how that will work, but I'm tired now. The sun's only just going down, but I think I'll go to bed.

Not tomorrow

It took three days to make something vaguely resembling a shelter. It's not that I didn't work hard but I get tired so quickly. That's a little better now that I have fish again. I spent a whole morning floating gently on my stomach, net at the ready, breathing through the snorkel and lying in wait. I caught four small ones and one that's as long as my hand. Who know what they are. Perhaps they're endangered species? Well, so am I.

I barely cooked the first two, I was so desperate to eat them. The bones are very soft, you hardly even notice them, and the eyes are tiny so as long as they are part of a bigger mouthful, you'd never even know.

I cooked the bigger one for a bit longer and scooped out the insides with a stick.

Eating the fish gave me more energy, so my new routine involves fishing as soon as I am awake, and then working on my shelter, then fishing again before doing a bit more work. Fishing is like resting, except when I start to cough and end up splashing about, scaring away all the fish. Just lying there on the water requires no effort, although I do have to be careful. This morning I had floated quite a long way from shore without noticing and it wasn't easy to get back.

The shelter is not really a shelter. I can't cut down branches and, even if I did, I have nothing to bind them together with. It's not as though this is a tropical jungle full of vines and creepers. I wandered about among the trees and bushes, until I found a group of bushes, about chest height, bunched quite closely together and partly sheltered by a couple of straggly-looking trees. I lay down full length in front of them and scooped out all the rotting leaves and sticks and beetles and spiders and general woodland stuff from beneath them. Every time an insect appeared with the sticks and debris, I threw myself backwards and waited at a distance until it had scuttled off. I used sticks to do the scooping, because nothing would have induced me to put my hands in there until I knew it was cleared.

When the ground beneath the bushes was clear, there was a space about a foot high and just about long enough for me to lie in, facing outwards, if I curled my legs behind me and let my feet stick out a bit. I told myself that I had frightened off all the insects. I needed to believe that. I covered the ground with several layers of leaves, mostly banana because they're the biggest. I also wedged as many banana leaves between the scrawny branches of the bushes as I could manage. There are no decent bananas left on the trees anyway, so I figure they'll be ok without their leaves. I need them more.

This took far longer to do than to write about. I had to keep stopping to cough and it's really hard to cough lying on your stomach. Also, my nose keeps running and then I have to back out of the bushes so I don't drip snot everywhere. And I was really thirsty, so I had to keep going back and filling up my shampoo bottle. Took me ages to wash it out thoroughly enough to use but at least it has a lid and it holds more than the juice cartons.

Every few minutes, I went back out onto the beach to check for boats. I can't help it, it's like having the lottery fantasy. I know the odds when I buy my ticket, but I still plan what I'm going to do with the money. I know the chances of a boat suddenly turning up are slim, but I have to keep looking.

The plan for my shelter is that, next time it rains, I drape both towels over the top of the bushes, lay the jeans on the ground over the banana leaves, put on as many clothes as I can manage and then curl up tight and wait for it to stop. I know I will be wet, but I'm hoping I'll be a lot less wet than last time. I will be protected by the bushes, then the towels, then the trees. Of course the ground will get wet, but it's very flat here, so the water shouldn't pool. I'm thinking perhaps I should also try and dig out a trench all round the area, so that the water will run into that, but that will only work if I make it lead away from the bushes, towards the sea. And that's a lot of work.

I've eaten a lot of fish over the last couple of days and my energy levels are better. Still coughing though. The olives are a lot more palatable after a thorough soaking and then a gentle roasting on the edge of the fire, so I've picked some more and they are soaking at the moment.

I have unscrunched some pages from the puzzle book, in case I run out of Jacqueline Wilson. I was going to do some of the puzzles, even though they're for children, but that would waste my pencils.

I used my hands to dig out a huge arrow shape on the beach, pointing to the place where I shall walk into the water. Just in case someone turns up while I'm out.

Displacement activity. Yes, all these things are probably a good ides but what I'm really doing is postponing the moment when I walk into the sea and start to swim. It's like leaping off a cliff and not knowing how deep the water is.

Tomorrow I will go.

Today's the day

Didn't sleep well. Coughed a lot, and had those weird dreams that happen when you're not well. Mostly, trying to button up a duvet cover and not being able to line up the buttons with the holes.

Went fishing first thing. Caught, cooked and ate two tiny silver fish and one medium sized brown one. I wish there had been more, because I don't know when I'll eat again. Put some olives into the edge of the fire and will eat them just before I go.

Not sure how far I will swim or how long it will take, so I would like to take water with me. The shampoo bottle is best, so I have filled it, but then I didn't know how to carry it. I can't swim with it in my hand, I'm bound to let go. Finally decided to put it into the rucksack and wear that. It will drag a bit, but I can't think of anything else to do. That made me wonder what else I could take with me that might be useful. I put a razor in, and then the nail scissors and reading glasses. And the snorkel and mask.

I really want to take the fishing net, but it's too big at the top to put in without maybe breaking the stick. I could find another one to thread through if it breaks, but this one feels lucky. God knows why.

I have nothing to wear. Don't laugh, I know it sounds as though I have a hot date or something, but I really have nothing to wear. When I'm fishing I don't wear anything because my knickers slide off me now, and my bra sort of hangs below me. The t-shirts just drag me down and everything else is so enormous that I would drown.

I can't set off naked, though. What if I find people? What if I get washed up somewhere else, and I don't have any clothes?

How long would I survive with just a rucksack, a razor and a pair of nail scissors?

Eventually, I packed my knickers, bra and a t-shirt into the rucksack. Obviously, they'll get wet, but they will still be clothes. I will swim naked, but I'll be able to make myself slightly more decent if I get out of the water.

I'm going to put this book into the suitcase now, and leave it in the middle of the beach. If the boat people come back, or the cavalry arrives before I get home, they will know where to look for me.

I've eaten the olives. They're still pretty horrible, but I can tolerate them. There's nothing left to do, no more excuses for not setting off.

I'm back

I've been back a couple of days, but I've mostly been asleep or fishing or eating. Will try and remember everything so I can write it all now.

I walked into the water, wearing nothing but the rucksack. It's a lot more comfortable now than it was when I first found it. I suppose that has something to do with all the weight I've lost. It wasn't heavy at first, but once I started to swim and it absorbed water, it began dragging. I swam out far enough to get clear of the rocks and then turned parallel to the rock face and set off. After only a few strokes, I was tired and wanted to stop, to turn back, give up. Why on earth did I think I could do this? It took three days to make my shelter and almost a whole day to dig my most recent toilet. I've hardly slept for days because of my cough. And now I think I can swim all round my island? Or to Greece, or home or something. Where *did* I think I was going? Why was I out there?

I told myself I would swim ten more strokes and then turn back if I couldn't see anything promising. When I managed that, I decided to just do ten more. Perhaps by then, I would see something in the distance; land, a break in the rock face, a boat. Anything.

I kept on, ten strokes at a time, moving further and further away from my safe place and seeing nothing new. Sometimes, between the sets of ten strokes, I would stop and rest, floating gently on my back for a while. I would count to sixty and then start swimming again. Floating on my back wasn't great though, because the rucksack was much heavier that way round and I often found myself drifting back in the direction I had come from. But treading water took more energy.

The face of the cliff never changed. Solid, grey rock rose from the water, reaching for the sky. To be honest, it probably wasn't all that high, perhaps the height of two houses, but two or twenty, it made no difference. There was nowhere I could have got a handhold, nowhere I could have climbed up, or even rested on a ledge.

At least breast stroke is gentle. The sea was calm and I moved slowly on through the water. After a while, I didn't feel the need to stop any more, except when I had to cough. I just zoned out and my body took over. I swam on. And on. It felt like a million miles, but the waves seemed to be going in the opposite direction and it might only have been a couple of metres. Once or twice I shook myself out of my daze and turned to look behind me. I couldn't see my beach, couldn't tell where the rock face ended. In some ways that was encouraging. After all, I *knew* it was there, which just meant it wasn't easy to see from this distance. That could mean there was another beach just up ahead of me that I couldn't see yet. So, with every stroke, I lifted my head and checked, in case I had suddenly arrived.

Nothing. Then more nothing. And I was so tired. Also, I was getting cold. When I walked into the water it had felt warm but now, probably because I was moving so slowly, I was getting chilled. The sun was still shining, but somehow it wasn't warming the water around me. My fingertips were wrinkled and I was shivering.

Now and then I would realise that I had drifted further away from the rock face and would have to change direction to get closer. That took a lot of effort. I wondered whether I had really come as far as I thought. Surely if I had, I would be seeing something different now?

I was thirsty. That's when it occurred to me that, in order to get to my water, I would have to take the rucksack off and open it. So many things could go wrong. I could drop the rucksack as I took it off. I could manage to hang on to the rucksack but once it was open any of the contents might float out and away. I might struggle to get it back on again. I could drop the water bottle, or just the cap from it. Any of those things would be a disaster. How had I expected this to work? I really didn't know, but perhaps I had thought that, by the time I needed a drink, I would be on land again somewhere. I could have cried, but I didn't have the energy.

I started to cough hard again and found myself splashing about and swallowing half the ocean in an attempt regain control of my body. My stomach muscles were starting to hurt from the effort. Again, I considered turning back, but it was like waiting for a bus or changing queues in the post office. You just know that the minute you walk away from the bus stop or move to the shorter post office queue, the bus will turn up or your original queue will melt away. If I turned back, I would never know whether, just a few metres on, I might have found my salvation.

When the coughing stopped, I swam on for a few metres, but I was really struggling. To be honest, the main reason I didn't turn back was that I wasn't sure I'd make it all the way.

Then I saw something that finally gave me hope. Ahead, there was a split in the rock-face, a fissure. It didn't look very wide, but I headed towards it anyway, metaphorically crossing my fingers, which were actually so cold that I could hardly feel them any more.

Close up, there was nothing helpful. The split was about a foot wide and went back quite a long way. The face of the rock was smooth and there was nothing I could grab on to. I looked up as far as I could, willing the rock to suddenly reveal hand and footholds, a way of climbing to the top. Nothing. I considered sliding in and then trying to push myself up out of the water by pressing my shoulders against one side and my knees against the other, but there was no chance that would work. It was too narrow for me to get any leverage and, if I was realistic, I didn't have the energy for something like that. And, to be honest, I am not Indiana Jones. This time, the tears fell feely.

I was cold by then, and so very tired. I swam slowly away from the rock and a few metres further on, sniffing and coughing and then, at last, things looked up. There was another, much wider fissure in the rock, wide enough for me to swim in between the rock faces, without touching them at all. I allowed myself to hope.

Good and bad. The good was the fact that there was a tiny shelf of rock inside the fissure, even a smattering of sand, like the smallest beach in the universe. It wasn't even long enough for me to lie full length, but it was big enough for me to pull myself up out of the water onto, so that I could take off the rucksack and finally have a drink.

The bad? There was nothing else. Absolutely nothing. The fissure only went back about ten feet and the rock was sheer, no cracks, no waterfalls, no hand or footholds, and it was narrower close to the top, so very little sunlight was getting through.

I was too exhausted to think, to make a decision. I curled up into a ball, arms wrapped firmly around the saturated rucksack, and, in spite of the coughing, the cold, hard rock and the pain in my chest, I slept.

I woke, stiff and sore and coughing. It was daylight, but I had no way of knowing whether this was the same day, or I had slept through the night. I had been dreaming about seagulls flying over me and dropping fish. I could only eat them if I could catch them in my mouth as they fell, but when I tried to run towards them with my face tilted up and mouth open, I slipped on all the fish lying on the ground and fell.

Lying there, working on bringing my muscles back to life, it occurred to me that I don't see birds on my island. I'm still certain that I must be close to people, but surely birds would drop in if I were that close? Something to think about another time. I reached out for the rucksack and that was when I panicked. At some point while I slept, I had released my grip on it and now it was nowhere to be seen. I dropped into the water and felt all around me, but there was nothing. I tried diving down but without the snorkel and mask I struggled and anyway, very little sunlight was making its way into the crevice and the water was dark. And so cold. So very cold.

All the activity made me cough again, and it started when I was underwater, so I came to the surface spluttering and gasping, spitting out saltwater and thrashing around wildly. I swam out into the open water, where it was slightly warmer, then let myself give up. I just floated. Every part of me ached and my brain was spinning. All my most precious things had gone. I had no idea whether I would be able to catch fish without the mask and snorkel. My underwear wasn't a big deal, but the reading glasses and scissors had gone too. These things that I had lost were the closest I was ever going to come to goats and chickens. And they were gone.

I knew I couldn't go further forward, so I started to head back. Slowly, so slowly. I wasn't exactly swimming, I was more sort of floating along, occasionally adjusting my direction with an arm. The sea seemed to be moving in the direction I wanted, but now and then I found myself drifting away from the rock face and having to swim properly for a while to get back on track. My mind wandered. I might have slept.

Caitlin swam beside me for a while, but I knew that couldn't be right, because she can't swim. She hates any water that's deeper than her knees.

A huge pink ocean liner went past and all the people waved and cheered me on. When I looked down I was wearing one of the bibs that athletes wear and I wasn't swimming, I was running through the water, but it was like treacle and I had to pull each foot up high every time I took a step, to release it from the goo.

A school of dolphins swam alongside me and called to me in squeaks and whistles. I wanted them to tow me to safety, the way Flipper would have done, but when I tried to catch hold of one of them, it's dorsal fin was razor-sharp and my hands were sliced open. When the dolphins saw the blood, they shot away, leaping and diving into the distance, and, from the other direction, I saw far more scary fins approaching. Dozens of them.

At that point, a horrendous cramp in my calf jerked me awake and focused, as I struggled to release the muscle and stay afloat with my head out of the water, coughing hard with the exertion. The sharks vanished.

I looked around and saw how far I had gone from the rock face. I wondered whether it would be better to just let go, drift away. I coughed harder and saw tiny flecks of red in the water in front of me.

I was so tired, I just wanted to give up, sleep, anything to stop the pain in my chest and the weight in all my limbs. Then I remembered Min. She was all alone in the suitcase, in the dark. And I thought about Dan and Ellie, Caitlin and Sam. At least, if my body was found on the island sometime in the future, they would have closure, they would know what happened to me, could have a funeral or something. If I float away now, they will never know, never be certain.

I held them in my head as I pushed myself to swim back in the right direction.

Held Dan's serious face, tongue protruding slightly between his teeth as he concentrated on icing the celebration cake when Sam and Caitlin opened their second-hand bookshop after three years of business planning and negotiations with the bank.

Held Ellie, insisting that "Mum, of *course* you need to take the travel iron. And the hairdryer. What if there's some gorgeous man in the group and you get to go out with him? You won't impress him in a wrinkled up frock and tatty hair." It was a waste of time pointing out that, as far as I knew, there were two men and six women in the class and, if either of the men was gorgeous, there would probably be a queue and I would be at the back. In Ellie's eyes, I am beautiful and all men should be falling at my feet. Love her. Love them all.

Heard the twins laughing so much that Ellie started to choke and we had to thump her on the back. That was when Sam had made the mistake of allowing Caitlin to cut her hair. It cost a lot of money to get that put right, but the photos still reduce us all to crumpled, giggling messes.

There's a photo somewhere, of me, Ellie and Dan all standing on the sofa, holding onto one another. The twins were about eleven. Caitlin was falling about laughing as she took it, so it's a bit blurry. I have my phone in my hand. That's because I had grabbed it as we all leaped onto the sofa, screaming at the sight of the largest spider in the world, just sitting in the middle of the carpet, watching us. I called Caitlin at work and she told her boss there was a family emergency and came to rescue us. She never let us forget it. I tried after that, to find away to deal with this stuff by myself. Went on eBay and looked for one of those spider-catching gadgets where you're at arms-length from them while you manipulate the handle to open and close the catchy bit. The trouble was, I couldn't look at any of them, let alone buy them, because all the boxes and all the adverts had pictures of enormous spiders on them. So I gave up. I know it makes no sense, I don't need to be told that they are more frightened of me than I am of them, but I can't help it. I feel this way about anything with more than four legs or with no legs. Beetles, spiders, snakes, slugs, worms. They all freak me out. I can't even touch a photograph. As I floated, I allowed myself a moment of pride for the way I had cleared out the space to make my nest under the bushes. Ok, I did leap back every time I saw movement, but I managed far better than I might have even a few weeks ago. That's what living on an island does for you.

I was drifting too much. Made an effort to focus for a while and move towards my goal.

Saw a bird. A real bird. It was a kingfisher. At least, I think it was. Tiny, sparkling blue-green miracle, darting along the top of the waves, close to the shore, moving so quickly that it might have been a laser-pointer and not a bird at all. That's when I realised that I could see the beach and had actually swum past the end of the rock face and started going round, following the beach towards the other end of the island.

I was so very happy to drag myself out of the water and onto the sand, but horrified to find that I couldn't stand, I just collapsed into a heap. I couldn't feel my feet at all, they were just pale, weird appendages hanging from the ends of my legs. I sat on the sand, rubbing the life back into them and screaming hoarsely as the feeling started to come back. That made me cough and, again, I saw flecks of red shoot from my mouth. I crawled across to the waterfall and lapped water from the wall. It didn't occur to me to open the suitcase and take out a juice carton or the shower gel bottle.

The sun was high in the sky and I lay, eyes closed, allowing it to gradually work its way into my bones. It took such a long time to warm up and I probably dozed, but I was reaching a point where the difference between waking and sleeping wasn't that great. It was hard to know what was real. Except the pain. That was very real and, although my muscles were warmer and looser, my chest felt as though someone had pushed a barbecue skewer into it. Every time I moved, the skewer stabbed something inside me.

Can a cough break your ribs? God knows. Once again, I was so aware that I am the wrong person for this. I should not be here. I know a million things about doing maths homework, I know how to paint a sunset and how to mould little animals from clay. I know how to make the best soup in the world and how to comfort a sick child. I know everything there is to know about re-upholstering old furniture. I know the best places to hide Christmas presents and the worst places to go on dates. I know (well, most of the time) when to comment on Dan's girlfriends and when not to. I know exactly which clothes will look best on Caitlin. I know so many things.

I don't know about coughs that make you feel as though you've been stabbed in the chest. I don't know which of the random bushes here it would be safe to eat the fruits from when all the bananas and pomegranates are gone. I don't know whether I shall be able to catch fish without the snorkel and mask. I don't know what spitting blood means, but it can't be good. I don't know a faster, less painful way to make fire, that doesn't result in blisters and splinters and broken nails. I don't know whether I will ever go home. I don't know how to survive.

Once I was warm, I pushed myself to my feet and opened the suitcase. I pulled on a t-shirt and tied it with the phone charger lead. I put the baseball cap on too, and I gave Min a hug and sat her on the sand. I couldn't decide which was more important, catching fish or building a fire. I thought about writing, getting the whole experience I had just had down onto paper, but decided I should eat first.

I went in among the trees and found a couple of squishy bananas, a pomegranate that had been lying on the ground but looked ok and a lemon. There are still plenty of lemons but I've been putting off eating them. The vitamins will be good for me but I can't get my head round the idea of just eating a lemon. So far, I have been squeezing the juice into water, and then drinking that. So I probably haven't got scurvy.

I ate the bananas and started on the pomegranate, but was eating much too quickly. Threw up. Not helpful. Buried the vomit in sand, washed my mouth out and then, very slowly, ate the rest of the pomegranate. Didn't throw up. Squeezed some lemon juice into water and drank it. Slowly.

Walked into the water with my fishing net, took a deep breath and lay on my front, forcing my eyes open, even though they didn't like it. I could see the fish but I couldn't stay underwater long enough for them to get used to me and come close. Moved further out and sat down, water up to my chin, holding the net beside me at arm's length. I could see the tiny fish, darting around close to me, but the bigger ones are usually further out. It took forever to catch four of them and I couldn't wait to get the fire going, so I just ate them. Oh, really? You think that's disgusting? So did I, once.

I kept flashing back to Ellie and her insistence on me bringing the travel iron. She was so certain it was the most important thing in my suitcase and I sort of feel that finding one in the suitcase from the plane must mean something. But I can't iron my way out of here. And there's no electricity anyway. If I could get it hot, perhaps I could use it to start a fire, but in order to get it hot I have to have a fire. Is that one of those paradoxes like, if you go back in time and kill your parents, then you won't have been born so you couldn't have gone back to kill them? Who cares?

I curled up on the beach, pulled the towels over me and slept again.

Dreamed about lightning striking my island. All the rocks were on fire. Min was singing Greased Lightning and her one remaining ear was on fire.

Dreamed that someone was smearing honey all over my face. Woke up with my nose running but, when I went to wipe it away, it was blood. A nose-bleed. What else can happen, what else do I have to deal with? Tipped my head forward, pinched the bridge of my nose and waited. There's a lot of waiting involved on an island. There's blood all over my t-shirt but the bleeding stopped eventually.

After it stopped I went over to the suitcase and picked up the iron. Something was bugging me. There was something I knew, but it was hiding in the place at the bottom of my brain, the one where words go to have a nap until you need them again, and brilliant ideas go because you haven't done anything about them.

Got my sticks and stuff out and started to make the fire. And then I had it. So simple. So obvious. How many fucking days, weeks, months have I been here? All this time, farting around with ways of making fire. Took me forever to work out the first method, with the reading glasses. The right person would have known, the moment they saw the glasses. Then, later, hours of pain, blisters, splinters and broken nails working out how to do it with sticks and then even longer for this to finally occur to me. *I am not the right person for this!* I should not be here, there's been some terrible mistake. There are a billion people better suited to surviving on an island, a billion people who may not be able to do maths homework or paint a sunset but who *can* make fire at the drop of a hat, catch huge fish, build shelters out of nothing, climb a sheer rock face. Save themselves. Where are they now?

Saw a ship, on the other side of the universe. I don't bother trying to attract their attention any more. I'm seeing thousands of tons of metal as a tiny spot on the horizon, so they will never see me. The same applies to planes.

Picked up the iron and the kindling and headed for the nearest dry rock, away from the water. Built a nest of kindling right up against the rock and added a sheet of paper from the puzzle book. Look at me, casually tearing up and burning books, equally casually writing all over them. Goes against everything hammered into me throughout my life. What would Sam say, sitting in the bookshop, tenderly fixing torn pages and broken spines, preparing her babies for their new homes, if she could see me now?

Took a firm hold on the iron, and brought it down hard, scraping along the rock in a downward motion, towards the kindling. And sparks flew. Of course they did. They would have flown weeks ago if I hadn't been so hopeless.

Had to rearrange the positioning of the paper and kindling a couple of times, but this was such an easy way to make fire. I could have been doing this since the beginning. Sparks do fly wherever they want to though, and I have a couple of tiny burns on my arms and some singed hairs, but who cares?

Once the fire was built, I sat down to write this. Should really go and check out my shelter and also catch some more fish but I'm so tired. Will sleep now and do stuff tomorrow.

X

Woke up coughing. Nothing new. Chest still hurts; think there's another skewer in me, as the sharp bit is in two places now.

Dragged myself into the water for fish. It's so much harder without the mask and snorkel, it took me ages to catch three tiny little silver ones. I didn't really feel all that hungry anyway, but I tell myself it's important to eat. Drank some lemon juice and water. Throat hurts from all the coughing. Honey would be wonderful but that would involve bees. I am very fond of bees, but not in huge quantities and not close up. Warm water would probably be soothing too, but all my containers are plastic or cardboard. There's nothing to heat the water in.

Put a clean t-shirt on, but couldn't be bothered to wash out the other one. The toilet's nearly full again, but I don't know if I have energy to dig another one today. The truth is, each time I dig one it's a bit shallower than the last. It just takes so much energy, digging with my hands, or a stick, scraping around tree roots and rock. Maybe I could just go in the sea, but that feels wrong, although I couldn't tell you why. Still, tearing books and writing in them used to feel wrong too. It's only a matter of time and perspective.

It's a bit cloudy today, so I went to check out my shelter, in case it rains later. I thought I might need to chase out a few insects. Maybe even a gecko. They are beautiful but I can't imagine cuddling up with one.

It looked fine as I approached, the banana leaves that I had forced in between all the branches were still there, and the ground still looked clear just in front of the bushes. I lay down so that I could roll inside, and found myself wondering if there was some way of letting more light in without letting in the rain as well, because I couldn't really see inside. Perhaps that was because it's cloudy today, but suddenly, I didn't like the idea of lying there in the dark. Then my brain kicked in and I worked out that, as long as I was facing outwards I would be able to see, it was only dark because I was looking inwards.

So I rolled myself carefully inside. It only took one full roll, because the space didn't go back far, but I decided that, when I actually needed it, I would put more clothes on, because small sticks and twigs were scraping my legs and neck. I thought maybe, instead of draping both towels over the top, I might roll myself up in one. That would be nice. Comforting. At first, I didn't plan to stay in there, just wanted to make sure my little nest was still there, really. Once I'd rolled in, I wriggled back a bit, to get myself as far away from any potential rain as I could and see how it felt. Even the small effort involved in getting down there and wedging myself in had worn me out. I thought perhaps I would just stay there and sleep for a while.

And then I heard it. Something was moving behind me, rustling in the bushes. Not an insect, unless it was some kind of mutation from a horror movie, something much bigger. The bushes rustled and moved behind and above me. Maybe there was more than one? Or, whatever it was, it was enormous. How could it be right behind me and also above me? I kept very still, telling myself it was probably a gecko. After all, I've seen no other animals here. If I moved a bit and made some noise, it would be frightened off. But what if it wasn't a gecko, what if it was something more aggressive, something that wouldn't run away but would attack if it thought I was a threat?

I needed to cough. I needed, very suddenly, to pee. I needed someone to take my hands and pull me from my nest, put their arms around me and tell me everything was going to be ok. To lift me up and carry me to a warm, soft bed and tuck me in. Next to the bed there would be a little table with a jug of cold, clear water, a clean glass tumbler and a box of tissues. There might be a bowl of fruit but I really wasn't that hungry so the fruit was optional. I needed someone to save me. I wasn't even capable of deciding whether to keep still or move, whether to roll out of my nest or to stay and wait for whatever might come.

The decision made itself. As I lay there, facing out towards the light, something slid slowly down from the bushes above my head, to hang in my line of sight. I have never moved so fast, even when I was healthy and fit. I have never been so terrified. There is no spider or beetle that has ever generated this mindless terror in me. Writing this now, I am shaking again and my writing's wriggling all over the place. Can't get it out of my head. Snake, snake, snake. When I close my eyes, the snake's tail hangs in front of them, brown and smooth. In another time and place, perhaps in a photograph, seeing those colours and patterns (without the actual snake), I imagine I might have seen beauty in them, but right then, lying under the bush, with no way out that wouldn't involve contact, all I saw was a monster.

As I threw myself forward and out, scrabbling on my hands and knees to get as far away as possible before turning back, my t-shirt was dragged up by the branches, exposing my back, and I felt the smooth, warm skin of the snake slide along my lower back and legs. Even then, in my panic, I was confused. I'd expected slimy coldness but the snake was warm and dry. That didn't change the way I felt about it though.

I reached a tree, several feet away from my nest, and turned back, ready to run again if necessary. All I saw was a flash of the snake's tail as it disappeared into the undergrowth. I never even got a clear idea of its girth or length. Not that it mattered. It was a snake and it had been sleeping in my bed.

I slid to the ground, and just sat, back against a tree, coughing and shaking, until my mind's eye showed me an image of a snake winding itself down from the tree directly above my head, fangs flicking in anticipation. I threw myself to the side, scraping my legs on the undergrowth, and looked up. There was nothing there, of course, I've watched too much Tarzan and Indiana Jones. But I couldn't stay among the trees a moment longer.

I made my way out onto the beach, constantly looking all around, up in the trees, down at my feet, terrified that I would stand on the snake or it would drop on me from above.

As I sit here writing this, I am trying to get my breathing and my imagination under control. I tell myself that this is the first time I have seen a snake, so there can't be many and they are probably scared of me, which is why they have stayed hidden. I tell myself that, although I could never shelter from the rain in my carefully prepared nest, I can still go in amongst the trees to find wood and food and to dig and use toilets. Nothing will drop from above as I walk, or slither out from a freshly dug toilet, just as I crouch above it. Nothing will slide silently out of the bushes to wrap itself around my ankles as I reach up to pick the last of the pomegranates. Nothing will hurt me.

I also tell myself that, even if there is only one snake on this island, which is extremely unlikely, I will never, ever walk into the trees again. There could be a million snakes in there and I have frightened one, so they will be out to get me. I have no idea what kind of snakes live here or whether they are poisonous. My back and legs are itching and I start to convince myself that the snake has somehow poisoned my with its touch. Going for a swim, to get it all off me.

Ok, back now. I know it's stupid, of course I wasn't poisoned, but I could still feel that smooth, warm body on my skin as I sat here and the feeling has gone now that I've been in the water.

I have tried and tried to go back into the trees. I won't survive here if I can't do that. There is no other shelter when the weather gets bad and, although there's not much fruit left, I need everything I can find. I went in a little way, once, and picked a couple of lemons, but then I heard something and hurtled out. I don't know what made the sound, perhaps it was in my head but, however hard I try, I can't go back.

I might feel better about it tomorrow. Meanwhile, when I need the toilet I am going into the sea, and I'm not that hungry so I'm just drinking lemon juice and water.

I was exhausted by the time I'd finished writing that stuff, so I curled up in the towels on the beach and slept. By the time I woke, it was dark and the fire was out, but I was thrilled at how quickly I could get another one going, using the iron. In the firelight, I can see that there are spots of blood on my t-shirt and on the towels. I must have been coughing in my sleep. Glad it didn't wake me, I'm so tired. I wish I could sleep forever.

Maybe four days later?

Every day I have tried to make myself go and look for fruit, but I can't get past the edge of the trees. I pull wood for the fire from the trees and shrubs closest to the beach, but even that terrifies me. What if I disturb a snake or, worse still, a nest of snakes? Do they have nests? Are they gregarious or do they live alone? Do they live on the ground or in trees? Are they nocturnal? I know nothing about them except that they instil a primal terror in me and no amount of common sense will change that.

But I must have fire and for that, I must have wood. I've taken to holding the iron by its lead and whirling it round and round over my head, then bringing it crashing down among the branches along the edge of the beach. That way, if there's anything in there, it will be scared off before I put my actual hands in. I scream and shout while I'm doing it too. I don't really sing any more. It's not essential and takes up too much breath and I have less and less of that.

Chasing the snakes away is exhausting and makes me cough so, once I have collected the wood and built up the fire, I sleep for a bit. Day and night have sort of blurred. The most important thing, the only thing that matters any more, is keeping the fire going. So, each time I wake, I chase the snakes and collect wood. If it's daylight, I try and catch a few fish before I go back to sleep. If it's night, I just curl up and go back to sleep. I don't sleep well and I dream a lot. My dreams are less clear now and don't remember them when I wake, I just know they were there.

Yesterday, I ate a fish and then found myself thinking I should have saved the head for the cats. Then I burned my finger while I was building up the fire, and turned to look in the bathroom cabinet for the Savlon. This morning when I woke, I reached for the notepad by my bed, to add toilet rolls to the shopping list. The world is blurring.

My cough is not getting better. There's a lot less sunshine than there used to be. I never feel hungry, although I force myself to catch and eat fish. Sometimes, I can't be bothered to cook them. It's only sushi, right?

Min is cross with me because I don't talk to her any more. She doesn't understand that I need all my breath for screaming at the snakes and for coughing.

I have seen a few ships in the last few days. Much too far away for them to see me. They probably can't even see the island, and why would they be looking anyway? When I can't sleep, I imagine the people on board.

Some of the distant blobs will be cruise ships. I see the people, in their best clothes, sitting around huge tables in the dining room, eating wonderful meals, drinking sparking wine, chatting and getting to know the other holiday-makers. I see them sunbathing or playing tennis on deck and casually glancing out across the sea, telling one another how beautiful it all is. If only they knew.

In my fantasy, some of the blobs are fishing boats. I like them better. They are crewed by small teams of men, skin browned in a way that a hundred years of lying on a beach in a bikini would never give someone. They work hard, (the details here are a bit hazy, I have no idea what deep sea fishing actually involves) and fall into deep sleep the moment they drop into their bunks at the end of the day. These men never look in my direction, they are totally focused on their work. When they dream, they dream of home, their families, their warm, safe beds.

Sometimes, I imagine a rescue ship, trawling the sea with special scientific equipment (again, the details are sketchy) searching for the place where the plane went down. They want to locate it, so that they can bring some closure to the families of the people who are still on board. This fantasy upsets me a lot and I always end up crying. If a ship does go out there with magic machines and tracks down the plane, if divers are able to get to it and bring out what's left of the bodies, if DNA testing is done to identify them, what will my babies think then? I'm not there. I'm not anywhere. I might as well be on another planet.

Each time I wake up, it's harder to get up, get moving, make myself do things. My chest hurts and there doesn't seem to be as much room for air in my lungs as there use to be. I draw in the biggest breath I can, but it feels like nothing. Every action leaves me breathless. I think I'm nearly ready to give up. I would love to just let go, to fall asleep and not wake up again. Never to have to chase snakes or collect wood, never to have to dig another toilet or even walk across the sand to the waterfall, to fetch water.

When I feel like this, I force myself to think of the effect my death would have on the twins. I make myself imagine their reaction when someone tells them that my bones have been found on a Greek island, that I am dead and they will never see me again. Of course, when I do this, they are still sixteen, they are exactly as I left them. But by now, they must be seventeen, their birthday is September 14th and that must have gone ages ago. And, by imagining them still the same age, I am also anticipating that my body would be found very soon after my death. It would be so awful if I gave up and died and a boat turned up the following day.

I must make myself keep trying. I still go the edge of the trees all the time and try to make myself go in. But every tree root and rotting branch is a snake and every sound, however tiny, sends me staggering back to my fire. I'm pretty sure snakes don't like fire.

I am catching far less fish now. I just don't have the energy to stay out there long enough. I tend to eat them as I catch them, because I'm only getting the small ones anyway and it's not worth the bother of cooking them. I'm quite good at bashing them on a rock to make sure they're dead. Or, if I'm still sitting in the water hoping to catch more, I just hold the net out of the water until they die.

I have decided to write letters to Ellie and Dan and Caitlin. There's nothing worth writing in this journal any more because each day is the same now. I chase snakes and collect wood, I fish, I eat fish, I take care of the fire, and I cough.

I would like to leave messages for the people I love, though, and if I don't do it now, I may never be able to. There are rainclouds in the distance and I'm not sure I will survive if they are heading this way. I shall write their letters separately. They are not for anyone else to read. I have several pages of My Sister Jodie left and some from the puzzle book, so I will use them and fold each letter up and write the name on the outside. Please don't open them unless they have your name on.

Eleanor May, my precious girl. From the moment you came into my life, exactly four and a half minutes before your brother (and you never let him forget that, did you?), you have held me in the palm of your hand. I would have given you the universe, if it had been in my power. All my plans about the way I would bring up my children, how I would be strict, not give in to tantrums, no sweets until they started school, no fussiness about food, all those things flew out of the window when you arrived.

You stole the hearts of everyone when you were tiny, with your wide eyes and ready smile. You had no fear, threw yourself into every new experience with an abandon I envied. On your first day at school, you hurtled into the classroom without even one backward glance, while I tried to hide my tears and behave like a grown-up. The day we took the stabilisers off your bike, you shot off into the distance, squealing with glee, and crashed straight into the dog poo bin at the side of the path. You got up, teeth gritted against the pain in your head and knees, and brushed away my hand as I reached out to soothe you. You wore those bruises, and many more afterwards, as a badge of honour.

At eight you were going to be a gymnast. You worked so hard, practiced all the time, cartwheeling and somersaulting round the park. You stopped because your school didn't have the resources or staff to take your training further and you were frustrated. You wanted to be a champion but all they could do for you was allow you to star in the end of term production.

At ten, you were going to be a famous showjumper. You had three riding lessons then gave up because it wasn't exciting enough. You were never one for patience. It wasn't good enough to understand that you have to learn the basics before you can do the hard stuff. After all, you never really walked, you always ran. You never sat still when you could be moving.

By fifteen you knew that you were destined to be a famous scientist. A Nobel prize by the time you were thirty, you said. Oh Ellie, sweetheart, never let go of that dream. Whatever happens to me now, whether I come home to you or not, keep working, stay focused, realise your dreams.

But while you're working, don't stop having fun. Miss your curfew now and then. Caitlin will try not to smile while she tells you off. Argue and fight with Dan, he can take it. And if you don't scream at him when he eats the last chocolate biscuit, he will worry about you.

Be kind to yourself. Never, ever, think that you were responsible for what's happened to me. Because I do know that this holiday was your idea. Well, not this holiday, but the one you planned for me. I know that Caitlin didn't think it was a good idea at first, she was worried about my fear of flying, thought perhaps I wouldn't go and then the money would have been wasted. You were insistent, you knew me better perhaps than anyone, even the sister I grew up with. You knew I would be so thrilled at the prospect of the painting but, even more, you knew how touched I would be at the idea. I could never let you all down by not going.

You helped me research phobia treatments, you were always home when I got back from my sessions, even on Thursdays when you would normally have been at Kelly's, working on your top secret science project. You helped me find the courage to get onto that plane and, in spite of everything that's happened since, I love you for that. Please believe me when I say that I have been ill and in pain and I have been afraid, but I have not for one moment thought that anyone was to blame. I have no idea what happened to make the plane crash, but I do know you had nothing to do with it.

Take care of yourself, my darling. Be happy. Live every second of your life. Regret nothing.

You are always in my heart

Mum.

I wrote Ellie's letter first because I know she will feel responsible. If, for any reason, I don't get them all written, at least she will know that she mustn't blame herself. It won't be that easy, I understand that, but in time, if she keeps reading the letter, she may get there.

Coughed quite a lot while I was writing the letter, and there are tiny specks of blood on the paper. Licked my finger and tried to smudge the specks as much as possible so that it's not obvious what they are. It's supposed to be something to remember me by, not some kind of horror prop. Was exhausted when I'd finished writing Ellie's letter, so I went to sleep.

When I woke up, it was dark and the fire was going down. I threw a few branches onto it, but there were no more left in my pile and I knew it wouldn't last the night without more.

This was a crisis. I can not be here without fire, it's the only comfort left. But there was no way I could go and collect wood in the dark. I paced backwards and forwards between the fire and the edge of the trees, trying to make a decision and becoming more tired with every step. In the end, I don't remember stopping and lying down, but I woke this morning with the sun high in the sky, in the middle of the beach, flat on my back. Not cold, I haven't really been feeling the cold so much in the last few days.

I had trouble standing up. Got there eventually, and staggered down to the water to wash my face and wake myself up properly. The fire was out and the ashes were cold. I wasn't strong enough to swing the iron properly, so I stood at arms length from the trees, ready to run at the slightest hint of danger, and reached out to pull twigs and small branches towards me. I had to stop several times, but eventually I had enough wood to get the fire going and keep it going for at least a couple of hours. I knew I would need to collect more before nightfall, but I wanted to stop and write Dan's letter. I would never forgive myself if Dan thought I cared more about Ellie than him.

Daniel James, my sweet son, I have missed you every minute since I walked away from you at the airport. You have always been the quiet one, never pushed yourself forward. When Ellie rushed in, you held back, you always let her take centre stage, allowed her to shine.

But you shone too, perhaps less brightly but more consistently. When Ellie was trying to run before she could walk, you were tottering along steadily and generally got there ahead of her. You always waited though, once you reached your goal, and shared whatever prize might have been waiting there.

While Ellie tossed and turned through the night, following her dreams, you could be found in the morning, exactly as I had left you the night before. You have always been the calm one, the one who arrived when you said you would, brought what you had said you'd bring, who remembered to take your P.E. kit on the right day, and reminded Ellie to take hers.

You were there to pick Ellie up when she skidded off her skateboard into a park bench, and she was there to see you the first time you stood alone on a stage.

We were all so proud of you last summer when you finally allowed us to see your GSCE artwork. You hadn't wanted me to know how amazingly good it was, because you thought it would make me sad. You, more than anyone, understood how much I lost when I let go of my dream of being an artist, because you have that dream too. Keep painting Dan, never give up.

Every day for weeks you went to the bookshop after school and helped Caitlin and Sam clean, mend, paint and organise, ready for the opening. You even coerced some of your friends into helping.

You made Ellie laugh through her tears when Tom decided he'd rather go out with some girl he'd met on holiday, by threatening to beat him up for her. He was twice your size. He played rugby, you play the clarinet. You have been Ellie's rock, and she will need that from you now, more than ever.

But sweetheart, you should never feel that you have to step up, take care of Ellie, take care of anyone. You will need to be there for one another, to be each other's rock.

You are a wonderful person Danny, and a wonderful artist, and you should never forget that. I miss you so much that it hurts.

Take care of yourself my darling,

Mum

By the time I'd finished writing Dan's letter, I was crying. There hasn't been a day since I woke up on the beach when my children haven't been in my head, in my heart. For seventeen years, they have been the centre of my life, I have always known where they were, when I would see them again. The longest we have been apart was a couple of one week school trips. And now, I have no idea where they are, what they are doing or thinking. I may never see them grow up, fulfil all their amazing potential, have children of their own. I might become a grandmother and not even know about it. Years from now, if I am still here, it will be like that cat in the box that might be dead. I will be a granny, or not a granny, unless I go home, and then I will know.

I might get home, of course, but right now, things are not looking promising. Once I'd pulled myself together a bit, I coughed my way into the water and managed to catch a couple of fish. I wasn't very hungry so I took the time to cook them. To be fair, they do taste a lot better cooked, but sometimes, I just can't be bothered.

Then I collected more wood. I don't have the energy to swing the iron at all, I'd thought eating the fish would help, but it didn't. At least it was light though, so I got as close to the trees as I dared, and pulled off as much of the easy stuff as I could, yelling all the time, just to scare off any lurking snakes. I am working my way along the beach doing this, so at some point, when I get to the other end, there will be no more branches in reach that are thin enough or dead enough for me to pull off. Not sure what happens then.

The rainclouds seem to have disappeared, thank goodness. It's never hot any more, but it's not really cold. It's just that I'm so thin now, that I have to wear all the clothes, just to stop myself shivering. Only a few days ago, the cold wasn't bothering me, but now I'm cold all the time.

I built up the fire then curled up to sleep for a while. When I woke, it was dark, but the fire was burning well. Coughed for a while and fell asleep again. Dreamed that I had forgotten to put stamps on the letters, and Dan and Ellie had no money, so the post office wouldn't let them read them.

Today, I am having trouble walking. My legs are wobbly and they don't want to hold me up. My stomach hurts. I know I'm ill, but can't properly define what's wrong. There's the cough of course, and the pain in my chest, and the wobbliness and weakness, but I don't know what that adds up to. Bronchitis? Pneumonia? Malnutrition? Just being very hungry and pathetic?

I lay on the sand and tried to think of people I know who would have managed this better than I have. Ellie of course, would have built a raft within the first twenty minutes, using nothing but the rucksack and a pencil sharpener, and sailed off towards home without a hint fear. If Sam didn't come back no-one would ever have known what happened to her, because she would never have been able to bring herself to write in the books. Perhaps Dan would have made himself a musical instrument somehow, and lured ships towards the island to save him.

Now my mind was wandering into strange places. The beach was crowded with people I have known through my life and they were all very busy, building rafts, collecting wood and fruit, catching fish, building up the fire. And, weaving amongst them, ignored by everyone, there were dozens of long, brown snakes. No-one seemed to mind the snakes, no-one was being bitten or running screaming. And there were kingfishers flitting amongst the people who were fishing. They seemed to be showing them where the best fish were. I could see that people were laughing and talking, calling out to one another; a group of young people from Ellie's karate class were playing volleyball, using Min as a ball. She floated through the air, not seeming to mind. Some people were singing. But I couldn't hear a sound, it was all done with the mute button on. I felt around, looking for the remote, so that I could turn the sound on, but I couldn't find it. No-one was looking at me or talking to me and I realised that I was a ghost, already dead, and that they couldn't see me at all. I shouted as loud as my throat would allow, to attract their attention. The shout, pathetic though it was, woke me from my dream-state and I sat, alone, and cried. I knew I had to write Caitlin's letter soon, or it would be too late.

A turtle swam past. I couldn't decide whether it was real or not, but I think it must have been, because it wasn't multi-coloured or singing or anything and everyone else had vanished.

This morning, when I woke, I felt a bit better. No idea why, but I'm taking advantage while I feel like this. I've built up the fire and caught and cooked eight small fish. I've only eaten three of them, and am saving the rest for later when I'm too tired to catch more.

I have filled all my water containers and half-buried them in the sand close to where I sleep, so that they don't fall over. If I am thirsty and too tired or ill to go to the pool or waterfall, I will have them. I've even washed out a couple of t-shirts that had blood on the front, but the stains are still there. I'm wearing the jacket over everything most of the time now, and there's blood on that too, but I'm not taking it off to wash it.

I don't want you to think I'm skipping about, full of the joys of spring. I have done all these things very slowly and it's the afternoon now. At least, I think it is, because there's no sunshine, it's very overcast. I can only really guess at time of day with any accuracy when I can see where the sun is.

Haven't seen anyone wandering about on the beach today. And no kingfishers or snakes. Also, Min is sitting exactly where I put her and is not taking part in any sports. Maybe I'm better? But the cough's still bad and the pain in my chest remains constant.

I've shouted at snakes a bit more and collected more wood. There's not loads, but enough to get me through until tomorrow, I think. There are two ships at the edge of the world. I picked up the longest branch from the fire and waved it, flaming, backwards and forwards above my head. They ignored me. From that distance, if they can see the flame at all, it probably looks like a cigarette burning. Or a dot, a pin-prick so tiny that they might not even be certain they've seen anything at all.

Today I am going to try again to go in among the trees and get more wood. I can't carry on like this, it's ridiculous. I saw one snake, when I'd been here ages. The chances of seeing another one, just a few days later, must be really slim.

Later

Well, I tried. First, I put on one of the pairs of jeans. That was hard work, because they are so enormous and I am so skinny now. They are also made for someone a lot taller than me. The waistband came right up to my boobs and the legs were miles too long. I rolled the top over and over, which sort of helped to make them a bit tighter, but I still had to tie the phone charger lead round tightly to keep them up. Then I rolled the legs up, but there was nothing to fix them in place with, so they kept dropping down over my feet. I really wanted cycle clips or something, to stop things creeping up inside the legs, but there's nothing. I couldn't bear the idea of going in barefoot, so I put the sandals on. They're massive on my size five feet, and keep sliding about, so I was walking in a sort of shuffle, trying not to fall out of them. I wasn't going to be able to run away from anything.

I stood at a place where there's hardly any undergrowth and I could see quite a distance into the trees. I looked very carefully, first up in the branches, then down at the ground, then up again, in case a snake had arrived wile I was looking the other way. There was nothing, not even an insect.

I stepped in. In fact, I took three steps. Then I stopped to look around again. My heart was beating so loudly, I figured the people on the ships should hear it and would turn up any minute to save me. My fingers were tingling and going numb. That's what happened in the first couple of sessions of phobia therapy, when I tried to imagine boarding a plane. The therapist said it was panic attack. Standing in the trees, I tried the exercises that had got me out of that room and onto a plane. I imagined my safe place, calm and quiet, restful. I closed my eyes and slowed my breathing. And then I really panicked. With my eyes closed, there could be snakes all around me, slithering, sliding, entwining around one another. They could be circling me, waiting to pounce. I had a brief moment of lucidity when I told myself that snakes don't pounce, but that didn't last because I realised that the word I really needed was *strike*. Snakes strike. Oh, shit. I was standing there, wearing an outfit that even Charlie Chaplin would have been embarrassed to be seen in, unable to move at more that a medium-paced shuffle, with my eyes closed, potentially surrounded by snakes waiting to strike.

I felt dizzy and couldn't remember which way I had been facing. I wanted to try to edge very slowly back out onto the beach, but what if I accidentally moved further in?

I opened one eye, very carefully, so that the snakes wouldn't see me looking, and was relieved to see that there weren't any. Not one. But I was looking down at the ground and they might all be hanging above me from the trees, waiting to wrap themselves around my neck or slither inside my t-shirt. I didn't look up to find out. I shuffled madly towards the beach, one hand clutching the jeans to stop them falling down and the other at my neck, pulling the t-shirt tight to keep out any marauding snakes, which took forever, even though it was so close, and then tripped over my own feet and fell headlong onto the sand. I crawled several feet further before getting up to look back. No snakes in the trees, but they were probably hiding now.

Sitting here, writing this, I know anyone would think I was crazy, but everyone is afraid of something. Think about the thing that terrifies you more than anything in the world. Bats, spiders, heights, wasps, water, dogs, mice, rats, thunder. I knew someone once who was scared of crossing bridges, even the really big ones built for trains to go over. Think of your thing and then imagine that, in order to reach everything you need to survive, you will have to face that fear and overcome it. You will have to walk through a nest of spiders, cross a suspension bridge strung across the grand canyon, walk into a cave of bats. Whatever it is, think about how that would make you feel. Perhaps you're braver than me and could overcome the fear, who knows? What I do know is that I can't.

Oh Caitlin, I'm so sorry. I know how much you love my children, but you never wanted any of your own. Even when we were small and played with dolls and teddies, mine were children and yours were policemen or doctors or teachers. You were never a mother. All your dolls drove buses. Your favourite teddy ran a shop, where we bought all the sweets and toys we wanted. And now, I know you will take care of my children as though they were your own. Thank you. But take care of yourself too, and of your relationship with Sam. Ellie and Dan will need you, but you need yourself too.

We have always understood one another, known what was going on, what we were thinking. Today though, I'm struggling to find words. There are a million things I want to say. There's practical stuff like telling you where I hid the birthday presents for the twins and where to buy the cheapest cat food, and there's important stuff like telling you that, although she would never want anyone to know, Ellie gets scared sometimes. She worries about the future, about responsibility, decisions. She's always been the one to leap without looking and she's afraid of what will happen when she has to grow up and be sensible. I think she believes she might lose herself. Please take care of her.

And please don't let Dan abandon his music or his art, however sad he is. They will save him.

There's a painting behind the wardrobe in my room. It's not quite finished, but if you're reading this, it never will be, so I want you to have it now. I started it the day after your bookshop opened. I sketched you and Sam, sitting together, watching the people wandering among the shelves. You were so happy, so in love, so proud of what you had accomplished. I wanted to hold that moment forever for you. I've been working on the painting in spare moments and in secret, so it's taken ages; I was going to finish it this winter and give it to you and Sam in March, for your eighth anniversary, but take it now. It's all I can give you.

I guess you and Sam will move into my place. Remember when I was buying it and we went house-hunting together? You loved my room, with the huge bay window and the amazing built-in wardrobes. You said you were going to come with me and live in the wardrobe, it was nearly big enough. Well, it's all yours now.

I know you hate to cook. The twins will love having you there, because there's nothing they like more than ordering a Chinese or Indian meal and curling up in front of the TV with it. Or playing cards, competing for the last banana fritter.

Caitlin, I have a sort of plan developing in my head. It's the only thing I can think of that could get me off this island and back to you all, but if I do it and it doesn't work, that will be the end of everything and I will never see any of you again. There is no chance that I will survive and you will probably never get this letter. I am putting it off because I'm so afraid, but there's nothing else left. I haven't mentioned it to Dan or Ellie. But I want you to know that, if I do this and it fails, if I die here, I was never trying to harm myself. I don't want to die, I want to come home.

I have to sleep now. Might try and write a bit more in the morning.

Goodnight Katie,

xx

Now that I've written all my letters, I feel that it's the end of something. I'm not sure what to do next. I'm still coughing a lot and every time I do, there's a sharp pain in my chest. It's not getting better but I don't think it's getting worse either. The thing is, although I'm not really hungry, I know I'm not eating enough and I don't know what to do about it. The water's not as warm as it was and just sitting there trying to catch fish makes me cold. I have to give up before I've caught enough, and then I have to run up and down to get warm, which uses up calories, so I need more food. It's a vicious circle. Sometimes, I can't even do the running and I just stand still and whirl my arms around, but even that tires me out.

Today, I decided to make myself walk right to the other end of the beach and I'm going to try and take some fire with me. This might be stupid because I have so little energy and, if I have two fires going, I will run out of wood sooner, but what if a boat passes within sight of that part of the beach and misses me because there's no fire? I don't know why I suddenly think a boat's going to come by; if it hasn't happened by now, it probably won't.

But what if it *has* happened? What if, while I was running away from invisible snakes, a boat came really close to the other end of the island? They might have been sightseeing, or scuba-diving or fishing, or just a bit lost. What if, every day since I moved to this end of the island, boats have gone past the other end of the beach? On the other hand, what if, when I was staying at the other end, boats were passing this end all the time? I can't be in both places and I did decide, ages ago, that I needed fire in both, exactly because of that. After the rain though, I lost my focus. And my energy. I forgot my plan and made a new one. Perhaps if I had stayed on track, I'd be home by now.

I'm obsessing, going round in circles. Can't decide what to do, where to be. I have almost convinced myself that, wherever I am, a boat is passing a different part of the island. Or, when I'm asleep, there's one passing right by me. I need to be at both ends of the beach and also in the middle. I need to be awake all the time. I should be making noise all the time. I need to have fire at both ends of the beach and probably in the middle as well.

I want to live. Sometimes, I am so tired that I want to just lie down and forget to get up again, but I am still getting up most days and fishing, trying to collect wood and keep the fire going, trying to think of ways to get away from here. I still keep doing these things, again and again, more and more slowly, it's true, but I haven't given up. Can't give up. Not yet, anyway. There is a way, I think. But it has to be the absolute last resort, when I am convinced that nothing else will work. Perhaps that's why I'm thinking about making another fire and the possibility of boats coming close? As long as I am still holding on to the idea of rescue, I don't have to take the risk. So far, even at my most desperate, I still have that tiny fragment of hope alive in my heart, that thing that says I can't possibly die here, I must get home, it's only a matter of time. There's always rescue or escape in the books and films, so it must be possible.

For the first time, it occurs to me that perhaps the reason that people don't just die at the end of the films and books is that it's not what readers or watchers want; they get invested in the characters, wanting them to survive. So, even in the most unlikely and unrealistic situations, they survive, build a yacht out of leaves and twigs, find a barrel and shoot up the inside of a volcano in it, flying out of the top to land in an Italian vineyard (or is that a different film, not an island at all?). They build signal fires on hilltops, but no-one says anything about getting to the top of a sheer cliff-face to build one.

If this were a book or film then, I would survive. So maybe what I need to do is think about how a writer would make that happen. I need to stop obsessing about passing boats and step outside myself (that's happening more often than I feel comfortable with now, anyway) and look at this from another angle. I need to float above the island, above myself, looking down and taking stock of exactly what's available here and what I am capable of. Then I can decide how a writer would rescue me. Then I can rescue myself.

It's not a book though, so it would be perfectly normal for me to die. It's not as though anyone has a vested interest in my survival, is reading my story with bated breath. I bet hundreds of people get washed up on islands every year and die, and it's not a problem because nobody knows. Well, not hundreds, but dozens. Some, anyway. It must have happened at least once. Somewhere, there's an island with the bones of a person who was washed up there and struggled to survive, find food, stay warm and healthy and eventually died regardless of all that effort. And nobody knows, so nobody cares.

I can't think like that, I need to be positive, keep believing that I have to be saved because I have never read a book or seen a film where, however bad things got, the hero didn't survive.

This is my new beginning. I've postponed making more fires and I'm going to look very carefully at every single resource available to me, one more time. I will focus and try to think laterally. A towel is not necessarily just a towel, a safety razor is not necessarily just a safety razor. I have to be imaginative, see things differently. I have to see potential, not restrictions. This is not easy because I am still obsessing about missed opportunities to attract passing boats, but I'm doing my best to be rational and accept that there probably haven't been any.

I started with the things that I have pretty much ignored. The Nintendo game thingy, the plastic hair band, the eraser and the pencil sharpener. I have used the sharpener on the pencils, but maybe if I could get the blade out, I could use it for something else? I laid these things out in front of me and looked at them. I wondered what I would think if I had never seen anything like them before, if I was an alien from another planet. What would I think they were for?

Nothing came to mind. There are batteries in the game thing, but I can't see what use they could be. There is absolutely nothing I could use the plastic hair band for and why would I want an eraser? It's hard enough to write all this stuff, without rubbing it out. I've tried thinking laterally. Nothing.

I looked at all the clothes next. The thing that stands out is that, although the orange towel is very grubby, it's still very orange. It could attract attention, if someone was close enough. I'll hold that thought. The rest of the clothes are grubby, stained and tatty. There are rips and tears in a lot of the stuff and much of it is stiff with sand and salt. I could make a scarecrow, but I've never seen a movie where a scarecrow rescues someone from an island. Still, it's a thought. Maybe I could leave a scarecrow at the other end of the beach? But them I'd have less clothes to wear, and I'd be cold.

There are the razors. They have been useful for cutting my hair, but they don't help with anything else. I did try scraping the skin off a fish with one, but it was useless and I gave up. I do however, occasionally shave my legs and armpits, just to cheer myself up. But that won't get me home.

There's what's left of the books. I have the three novels and haven't written in them or torn them, although it could come to that. I have this book, where I am rapidly running out of pages to write on, and I have a bundle or pages from the puzzle book and the other Jacqueline Wilson. However hard I try, I could not imagine a use for any of the books, except lighting fires. And then, just like that, I could. It had never occurred to me before but, after all, it wouldn't have been an option at first.

I wrote a note on a couple of pages of the puzzle book. No idea where I am, so just gave the flight number and some information about the island. And I told them about the canoes or kayaks or whatever they were. I said I was desperate. Then I put the note into the shampoo bottle and screwed the lid on tight. The bottle is clear plastic, so anyone picking it up will see the note. I walked out into the sea, then swam as far as I felt safe, clutching my treasure, turned to float on my back and threw it as far as I could, out into the ocean.

The bottle may never be found, but it's the first thing I have done that is really positive and actually aimed at trying to get myself rescued. Was tired from the swim, but feeling very proud of myself by then, and inspired to carry on looking through my stuff.

I went back to all the electrical things. Adapters, charging lead and iron. Well, I need the iron to make fire, and to attack the snakes with but I really couldn't imagine any other use for it. I guess if I caught a big fish, I could use the iron to bash it on the head, instead of leaving it to flap itself to death, but that's not essential and it won't get me home.

Looked at the adaptors, turning them round and round in my hand. Waste of time. There is absolutely nothing useful that I can do with them, there really isn't. I put them back into the suitcase.

I looked at the wash-bag and the hair gel, which is in a transparent plastic tube. I've never even opened it; doing my hair has not been at the top of my list of priorities. I've never used anything like that on my hair before. I wondered if it might be useful for anything else? Is it flammable? Could I have been using it to help get the fire going? Possibly, but I don't need it, the fire's fine now, as long as I can keep collecting wood.

I gave up. I have looked and looked and I am not inspired by any of this stuff. I even sat for a while and wondered what I might use Min for. And the baseball cap. Nothing.

Then I looked at natural resources. There's fresh water, which is very wonderful but I can't build a boat with it. There is some fruit, although a lot of it is rotting now and I can only get at it if I overcome my panic about the snakes. There's wood too but the same applies. Most of the trees are pretty straggly as well, so even if I had an axe or a saw and nails and stuff, I'm not convinced I could make a very successful raft. I'm not counting geckos as a natural resource. Firstly, I'd never be able to catch one and secondly, nothing would induce me to hurt one, even if I could. There's fish, and I am using them for the only thing they can really provide; food. I don't know what happens to fish in the winter. Do they go somewhere different? Or does the sea get choppier and make the fish harder to see and catch?

So, I have had one idea and sent a message off into the distance, but that's it. I was tempted to just sit on the beach and wait for rescue, but I know that's stupid. How many billions of gallons of water are there in the sea? How many miles is it to the nearest inhabited land, where my bottle could wash up? Let's face it, it was worth doing, but it's a very long way from being a guarantee of rescue.

I was very tired by the time I had been through all my stuff, even though I was mostly just sitting down looking at things. I curled up by the fire, and slept.

When I woke, it was dark and the fire was nearly out. I was cold, although I was wearing most of the clothes. I had a headache. I was hungry too, which was unusual. On the other hand, I was still far too tired to do anything about any of that, so I just tried to go back to sleep. The hunger and cold and my cough disturbed my rest though, and I fidgeted and wriggled about, trying to get comfortable, get some more sleep. I gave up around dawn and got up. My legs were wobbly again. I tried to remember when I'd last eaten, but I couldn't. I tracked down a cooked fish, wrapped in paper and packed away in the suitcase, and ate it, but it wasn't enough. It was a bit smelly, too.

I've started checking the sand all around where I sleep, every time I wake up. At the first sign of a snake trail, I will go into the water and never come out.

I needed to make a decision between fishing for more food or collecting wood and getting the fire going, but once again, decision-making seemed impossible. I kept wandering from the water's edge to the trees and back. Was I going fishing or collecting wood? In the end, it was the fact that I was so cold and would need to take my clothes off to go fishing that did it. I couldn't bear the idea of undressing, so I needed to start a fire.

I knew I was going to need to walk a long way along the beach to start collecting wood. There's hardly anything within reach close to this end now, and I'm not even going to waste ten seconds wondering whether I'm brave enough to go in amongst the trees.

Decided I might as well go back to my fire plan. I'm going to have fire at each end of the island and perhaps half way along the beach as well, and I thought it would be best to start with the one at the other end, just because there's more accessible wood there. If a boat comes past this end while I'm gone, they might see the suitcase and the thing with the sticks for drying clothes on. I draped the orange towel over it to attract their attention.

I filled a juice carton with water, put the baseball cap on, in case of sudden sunshine, grabbed the travel iron by its lead and set off. It took me ages, to walk to the other end. I wonder whether I miscounted the steps the first time; it felt more like a thousand today.

When I got there, I swung the iron at the trees a couple of times, to let the snakes know I'd arrived, and pulled out a few branches. Then I used the branches to scrape out some of the stuff on the floor; twigs, pine needles, bits that would be useful for kindling. Didn't want to stick my hands in there. I was so tired though. Couldn't think straight and definitely couldn't collect any more wood. As I curled up on the sand to sleep I realised I hadn't eaten anything before I set off and I hadn't thought to bring the fishing net.

I fell asleep swearing inside my head at my own stupidity and also at the universe, for selecting *me* for this experience, when there are so many others more qualified for survival than I am.

Woke up eye to eye with a gecko. I blinked first and it vanished in a flash of green and brown.

I was chilled through and I knew there would be serious consequences if I didn't get the fire started fast. I couldn't imagine walking more than a few steps feeling that way. I piled up the pathetic bunch of branches that I'd collected, ready for fire, then dropped the pile of kindling down by a rock and used the iron to light them. Every time that succeeds, my mood lifts and I am so proud of myself.

Once the kindling was alight, I didn't have much time, because there wasn't a lot of it. I stuck the end of a branch in and turned it gently until it caught fire, then took it over to the main pile of wood and used it as a torch. Thank goodness it caught quickly. I stood as close as I could get and warmed my legs, leaning forward to warm my hands and face too, but doing my best not to set my jacket alight. The sleeves are quite flappy, because it's too big for me and I don't want to attract a boat by setting my body on fire. As soon as my limbs lost their chill, I got hold of the iron and terrorised a few more snakes, collecting as much wood as I could before my legs started to turn to jelly again. Why on earth had I not thought about food when I was planning this?

I tried to give myself a good talking-to about the snakes. Told myself there might only be a handful, maybe even just that one. Perhaps it had already left the island. Do snakes swim? I have a feeling that some do, but maybe they are water snakes. Oh, my natural history knowledge is so inadequate. If I could win my ticket home by answering quiz questions about Michelangelo or the industrial revolution, all my problems would be solved.

It doesn't matter what I tell myself though. The fear is irrational and all-consuming. I've even woken up a couple of times in the night, terrified to open my eyes because I'm convinced that there are snakes all around me. Every time I wake, I check the sand as far as I can see, for slithery snake trails. Nothing. I told myself a few days ago that, if there was no sign of a snake for two days, it would be safe to go back into the trees. Then I thought I should give it one more day. Then one more. I can't go on like this, I will go crazy. I am already going crazy.

I got the fire built up hugely, warmed myself through and through, picked up a couple of branches that I'd saved and set off home, dragging them behind me. Slowly. Thought about how far it was and how tired I was and wondered what the chances were of me going back again to keep that fire going. My original plan had been to stop half-way back and make another fire, but of course that was out of the question. Just getting back here took all my energy.

The orange towel hadn't attracted any rescuers, everything was exactly as I'd left it. I thought about all the times I've yelled at the twins because someone's moved a book, a pen, my phone, and I can't find it. I would give anything to come back here and find that someone has moved my suitcase, written in my books, taken the towel down from the rack and folded it up. Evidence that I am not alone in the world. Not going to happen. And the way my brain is operating at the moment, I'd probably assume that the snakes had sprouted arms and legs and started invading my space.

I couldn't allow myself to rest. I took my clothes off, grabbed the fishing net and walked into the water. I was chilled through within minutes, but refused to allow myself to come out until I had seven small fish. Seven little fishies. Is that a nursery rhyme? If not, it should be.

Managed to get a fire started with the branches I had dragged back and then, still not allowing myself any rest, I took the iron with me and walked along to the nearest place where I could still reach breakable bits of tree and collected more. Dragged it all back to my fire and piled it on. And again. I forced myself through the other side of my exhaustion until I had a blazing fire and a pile of wood ready to feed it with.

Now, I'm warm and fed (and exhausted) and I can sit here and write and think. Did I tell you that, the last time I walked back with wood for the fire, there was a kangaroo hopping along beside me, telling me stories about people lost in the outback and something about dreaming? Each time it took a hop, it ended up miles ahead of me, but it stopped and waited for me to catch up. Can they swim, kangaroos? Could I have clung onto it and been rescued? Too late now, it's gone.

I think it might be time to give up. I don't mean time to die, I mean time to try my one last idea for attracting a ship, or even a plane. I still see planes quite often, but they're too far away to bother waving at.

Too tired to make a decision right now though, and it would need some preparation, so I will go to sleep and see how I feel in the morning.

Woke up coughing. Nothing new, but this time I just couldn't make it stop. It went on and on, while I pressed my hands over my ribs and tried to focus on holding my body together and drawing in some air between coughs. I was suddenly aware of just how prominent my ribs are now, I could count them, practically play a tune on them. Eventually, the coughing faded to the odd twitch of my ribs, and then it finally stopped. It's exhausting. Life is exhausting. Thinking is exhausting.

Today, I will leave this island, or die.

Wanted to say goodbye to the other end of the beach. That's where I first settled into a routine here, thought that I had come to terms with the fact that I was stranded, would be here for a long time. I was wrong though. Even now, when I'm ready to give up and try the most extreme measure I can think of, even now, I still think that any minute a boat will arrive. I will be picked up, wrapped in a warm blanket and carried gently to be placed carefully in the bottom of the boat and whisked away to safety.

I wanted to go back once more and say goodbye to the rock rooms, my first fireplace, the first fresh water I found here. Stupid, I know, given that I have so little energy. Perhaps I was just putting off the moment when I take the final step, reach the point of no return. Whatever. I was going.

Filled a juice carton, just in case, and set off. Walked slowly, a long way from the edge of the trees, constantly watching for snake trails on the sand. There was nothing except my footprints from yesterday. Was it yesterday? I'm never sure any more, how long I sleep for. My footprints were erratic and I could see that, at least twice on my way back, I had walked in a circle before lining myself up and moving on again in the right direction.

There was something bouncing about on the gentle waves at the edge of the the beach. Small, and far away, but as I approached it I was excited; it could be something really useful. No idea what; it certainly wasn't a goat or a chicken, but I needed a reason to hope and, seeing something new on my island gave me that.

Briefly.

As I got closer, I saw the shampoo bottle with my note in it, bobbing gently, a few feet from the shore. The lid was still on and the message looked dry, so I suppose at least I'd got that bit right. But here it was, not washed up on a holiday beach where a small child could take it to a grown-up and ask them to read the message, not pulled out of a fishing net, initiating an immediate radio call and a massive air-sea rescue operation, not discovered by a fishmonger as he cuts open an enormous fish and sees the stomach contents. It's here, on my beach, a matter of yards from where I last saw it.

I couldn't even be bothered to pick it up out of the water. I didn't finish my walk to the other end of the beach, I just turned round and walked back to the fire and the suitcase. Should have collected some wood on the way, but I had nothing with me to chase the snakes with.

This is the last thing I will write. Afterwards, if there is an afterwards, I won't need to write any more, or I won't be able to. Either way, this is the end.

I built the fire up a little bit, just enough to make sure it wouldn't go out, but kept a couple of branches aside. There's a ship on the horizon, a billion miles away, but I have to believe that's a positive sign.

I took off some of the clothes. I need to be dressed to stay warm, but the jeans and shorts and jacket will weigh me down if I'm in the water. I am wearing my knickers and a t-shirt, held up by the charger cable. Even now, when that gets wet, I have a brief flash of panic about water and electricity and the risk of electrocution. We are so thoroughly programmed.

I have put everything, even Min, into the suitcase. The only thing left out now is this book and the tiny stub of pencil I'm using. Min doesn't like it in the dark, but she will thank me later. I won't need the orange towel to attract attention, so that's gone in too.

I moved the suitcase as far from the trees as possible, without the danger of it being washed into the sea and I put the book and pencil down next to it. I picked up the longest piece of wood, held the end in the fire until it caught properly and then carried it, carefully, along the beach until the flames started to get too close to my hands. Then I walked towards the trees and held the wood out, close to the ground, so that the flames caught the undergrowth and small fires begin to sprout up. I didn't try and ignite the main parts of the trees, I had decided that the dead stuff underfoot would burn better to begin with.

I had to drop my stick because it had nearly burned away. I left it there, flames licking up around the base of a bush and catching the twigs and leaves above them, and I went back to my fire. I took the last stick, held it into the fire until it was well and truly burning, and then went back to the trees and pushed it firmly into a bush. Any snakes in there had just better move fast. I moved along a couple of times, igniting the undergrowth and small bushes in as many places as I could, until the stick was nearly gone, and my fingers were dangerously close to the flames.

I stepped back and watched for a while. It took a very long time for all the small fires to gradually creep along the ground and through the branches until they met and became one. Even then, the flames were low and gentle, until suddenly, it took hold. A small, scrubby pine tree went up with a whoosh and a shower of sparks. The flames were now racing to consume as many trees as possible, shooting skywards. Now and then there would be a loud cracking sound as a tree either split or fell, I couldn't see which. There was loads of smoke too, but I thought that was probably a good thing. Anything to attract attention. As the fire spread back, and I moved further away towards the water's edge, I could see that the smoke and even some of the flames were reaching higher than the cliff-top.

I had a moment of panic, when I imagined every snake, every beetle and spider and creepy-crawly that had been living in the trees suddenly making a run for it in my direction. I backed away until I was standing in the water, but even in my fear, the flames were mesmerising. And nothing came charging out of the trees, not even a gecko.

I had assumed that I would be safe watching from the beach but, as the fire grew, the heat became intense, even at a distance. I knew when I started this, that once it was done there would be no food or shelter left and, ironically, nothing to make fire with, but I had assumed I would be able to stay on the beach and watch the fire while I waited for rescue. Now, I new that quite soon, I would need to get into the water. My skin was burning hot, even though I was as far from the fire as I could get. Tiny sparks were landing around me and in my hair and I could smell burning as the hairs on my arms were singed.

There had been a gentle breeze all morning. I had assumed it would help to spread the fire, but I hadn't counted on it drifting the smoke in my direction. I didn't even see it coming, was completely unaware until I started to cough. I coughed until I thought I would throw up, tears streaming down my face. My eyes were stinging and my lungs were on fire. I had had no idea how fast fire travels or how genuinely painful it is to breathe smoke.

It was probably a bit late to develop a healthy respect for fire and smoke. You hear about people rescued from fires who suffer from smoke inhalation and you think, well that's ok, they're not burned and they're out of the smoke now.

It's not that easy. As the fire took a proper hold and raged through the trees, devouring everything in it's path, I felt as though someone had sandpapered my lungs and throat. I had moved back here by then, as far from the fire as it's possible to get, and was facing away from the flames, looking out to sea and trying to breathe in fresh air, but my eyes were still streaming and my lungs were raw. The fresh air didn't take away the pain in my lungs and throat and it didn't stop me coughing.

I realised I'd forgotten to collect some drinking water before I started, and I turned towards my waterfall and the pool, several feet from the nearest tree, thinking maybe I could get over there and drink some, but, through the smoke, I saw steam rising from the pool and the cliff-face. No water now.

So, I picked up my book and am writing this. If you're reading this and I'm not here, you need to know the fire wasn't an accident. I may be useless, the last person on earth who should have been asked to survive alone on an island, but even I couldn't set fire to the whole place by mistake.

I know I am close to people. I know that I am maybe a few hours away by canoe. Or kayak, or whatever. The people who live in the places the canoes come from would surely notice a huge cloud of smoke, would see the flames shooting into the sky. Wouldn't they? I know that there are ships on the horizon, that won't see the small flame of a beach fire, but must surely see an island burning. I know that planes go over regularly. Not directly above me, quite a distance away, but the passengers will be looking out of the windows, will draw attention to flames in the distance. Won't they?

The thing is, if no-one's looking, if everyone has better things to do, if they all think someone else has phoned the coastguard or the Navy or whatever, then this will be the end. There will be no food or shelter left, no wood for a fire. There will be nothing. I might catch a few more fish, but it will only be a matter of time before it's all over for me.

I have finally worked out how to make a signal. Somebody will see it. Somebody will come. I will put my book away in the suitcase now and I think I'll move out into the water a bit, because I'm very hot.

I have eaten the chocolate mini-roll.

All I have to do now is wait.

26752397R00078

Printed in Poland
by Amazon Fulfillment
Poland Sp. z o.o., Wrocław